Lorelei's Guiding Light

Lorelei's Guiding Light

An Intimate Diary

by

Lorelei Hills

As told to Beth Chamberlin

St. Martin's Press ❧ New York

This book is dedicated to all the past, present and future fans of *Guiding Light*. Thank you for being a member of our family. Congratulations on being part of history.

Acknowledgments

This book could not have happened without the hard work of a few wonderful people. First, I need to thank Mary Alice Dwyer-Dobbin for her support and for her dedication to this project. She successfully navigated this boat through some very rough waters. Secondly, Jennifer Weiss for her patience and intelligence. No other editor could have withstood the barrage of questions and changes. Thirdly, all the people at P&G, CBS, St. Martin's Press and *Guiding Light*, most especially Paul Rauch and Lucky Gold, who allowed this project to happen and who supported me along the way. Finally, my husband, Peter Roy, for working with me every step of the way. Without him, this project could not have been completed. I love you, sweetie, you are my personal guiding light.

Who am I?

I suppose this is a question most women ask themselves at one time or another in their lives, but usually when they do they're asking sort of a philosophical question. They're wondering who they really are underneath all the stuff: under their makeup and their smiles; under their attachments and obligations to family, lovers and friends.

But as for me, when I ask myself this question, I mean it in a very different way. I truly don't know who I am. I have no recollection of anyone or anything. I look in the mirror at my green eyes and my long auburn hair and I feel as though I have never seen this face before. I am pretty—or could be, if I wasn't so bruised and swollen. This is my one clue. I am black and blue all over. Something happened to me, but what? Maybe that's why I don't remember my past. Maybe I don't want to.

This diary will be my way of discovering my identity—at least that's what I hope and pray. I'll write as much as I can, as fast as I can, trying to use the bits and pieces that come to me to help me discover who I am and how I came to be here. This memory loss is a frightening thing. You don't realize how comforting a past is, even if it's a bad one, until you don't have one anymore. I can't move forward until I know where I've been.

There is something important in my past, something I need to know soon. Do I have a husband and children at home who need me? Am I in danger? I don't know, but whatever the answers to these questions are, I must be willing to face them. I believe my life depends on it.

This is what I know.

I woke up this morning in a strange bed. The bed was beautiful. It was white and deep and surrounding it on all sides was a curtain, a bridal veil of thin white gauze. I thought I could be in my wedding bed, only somehow I knew it wasn't marriage that brought me here. As I sat up, pain shot through me. I looked down and pushed the soft, cotton sheets from my naked body. Bruises spotted my legs and arms. A thousand questions sprang to my mind. How did I get here?

Who had undressed me? Had I made love to some man I couldn't remember? Was he responsible for these marks of violence that spread across my body?

I slipped from the bed to search the room for clues to my identity: something, anything that would jog my memory. The red terra-cotta tile felt cool beneath my feet in contrast to the warm breeze blowing in through open glass doors. The room was simple but elegant: White, scrubbed, plaster walls with a detailed swirl pattern on them. The ceilings were as high as a cathedral's, and sunlight flooded the room. A large tiled fireplace stood at the far end of the room; comfortable chairs flanked it. I walked to a mirrored wardrobe that stood to one side. This woman that stared back at me was beautiful. She had high cheekbones, emerald green eyes and full pink lips, memorable to everyone but me.

"I thought you would still be asleep," I heard him say from across the room. I whirled around to see a handsome, olive-skinned man with silky black hair standing in the doorway.

"You might want to cover up," he said as he gestured toward my naked body. I vainly attempted to use my hands to hide myself from his gaze. I turned to search for something to cover myself—a sheet, a piece of furniture, anything would do, but there was nothing closer than the robe he was holding. As he walked toward me, opening the robe, I let my hands fall to my sides exposing my full, round breasts to his appreciative stare. He circled behind me. He was so close that I could feel his breath on my neck. Did I know him? Had I made love to this man? He could be my husband for all I knew.

I froze, not knowing what to do.

"Your arms, señora," he prompted. I held out my arms as he gently slipped the robe over my arms and shoulders.

"My name is Roberto Octavio," he offered as he walked back around to face me. "And you are?" he said as he held out his hand.

I opened my mouth and struggled to speak, but what could I say? I had no answer for him. I had hoped he could unlock my memory. My hopes were dashed. I closed my eyes and looked to the floor, willing myself not to cry. I didn't want to appear weak in front of this man. But it was no use. Who was I kidding? I was vulnerable. I was with a strange man in a strange house in God only knows where and I had absolutely no idea who I was.

"I don't know," I heard myself answer him. Even my voice was foreign to my ears. I had an accent, a rather thick Southern accent. It occurred to me that this was clue number two. I must be from the southern part of the United States. But where? And where was I now? Every answer brought more questions.

"Where am I?" I asked.

He regarded me through dark brown eyes. I think he was trying to decide if he believed me. I can hardly blame him. What is it they say—"You can forget everything, but you never forget your name"? Amnesia: it seems like something someone would use as an excuse to avoid getting in trouble. Or to get out of trouble. And maybe that's what I was doing.

There it was again—that sense that I was running away from something or someone.

Finally his gaze softened slightly. "You must be hungry," he said as he took my hand and led me to a terrace outside the room. My eyes squinted as I attempted to adjust to the bright sunlight. Tropical plants were everywhere. Roberto, or more likely his gardener, had a green thumb. In the middle of this lush terrace was a table set with delicious food.

A maid was pouring juice. I heard Roberto say something to her in Spanish. I didn't understand a word. He could have been saying kill the American after breakfast for all I knew. As frightening a thought as that was, it did provide another clue. I hadn't been in this part of the world long.

As I looked at the food set before me, I suddenly

realized I was famished. I grabbed the rolls and began stuffing them into my mouth as fast as I could. I could feel Roberto staring at me. I think he was shocked or disgusted by my rudeness. For a moment I felt ashamed and in that moment I realized that it was a familiar feeling. Yes, I had felt shame in my life, but what had caused that shame I didn't know.

I put the rolls down. "I'm sorry," I mumbled. He just looked at me. Well, I couldn't stand the silence. I couldn't stand feeling like I was being judged. So I forced myself to be bold, to take charge of the situation. "You never answered my question. Where am I?" I demanded.

He smiled and in his smile he revealed part of himself. He was a man that knew women. He could read them. He could read me. I felt more naked in that moment than I felt without the robe. He could see I was scared and he could see my boldness was an act. But I wasn't about to admit that he was right. I turned away from him and pretended he was being tiresome. Then, for good measure, I shoved another roll in my mouth.

"San Miguel de Allende." He laughed.

"San Mig—what?" I asked through a mouthful of food.

"Mexico," he told me.

"Oh," I said, feeling embarrassed yet again. Had he

purposely waited to give me important information when my mouth was crammed with food? I'll get the upper hand on this man yet, I thought. Then I swallowed and pointedly dabbed my mouth with a napkin. I wanted to let him know that I could be just as much a lady as anyone.

"How did I meet you?" I asked with my most disapproving look. And there it was—that damn smile again. It was as if he knew every thought I had.

"Well, we did not actually meet until a couple of minutes ago, señora. I found you unconscious just outside my property last night. I brought you here to recover."

"Did you undress me?" I countered.

"Whatever else I may be, I am a gentleman. My maid saw to you."

Whatever else he may be. Well, there's a loaded statement if I ever heard one. Something about this man made me want to get up and leave as fast as I could. But something else about him made me want to take him back to that big, white bed, run my hands over his strong, tanned body, and take him inside me.

I forced myself back from my erotic reverie. "How did you know I was American?" I demanded. "I mean, here we are in Mexico and your first words to me are in English. That sounds pretty suspicious to me. Do you know something you're not telling me?"

"I know many things I am not telling you," he replied evenly, "but the reason I knew you spoke English was because you were mumbling in English when I carried you in."

"I was mumbling something?" I was filled with hope. This was it. He'd tell me what I was mumbling and everything would come flooding back to me. "Well, what was it?"

I waited expectantly for his answer. He hesitated.

"You were—" he began, but just then his cell phone rang. He answered; I waited. "Uno momento," he replied to the caller, and then to me he said, "I must take this call. I will see you this evening. Make yourself at home." With that invitation or order, I'm not sure which, he strode from the room.

"What was I mumbling?" I yelled after him. He didn't answer. He didn't even acknowledge my question. For a moment I couldn't move. I felt like I'd been punched in the gut. I couldn't breathe. He held the key to my past. How could he keep it from me? I got up and ran from the room yelling his name, but he was gone.

I wandered the house looking for him, looking for anyone. Everyone seemed to have up and disappeared. Were they hiding from me? Why wouldn't Roberto answer my question? What was I mumbling when he found me? Question after question that had no answer.

Soon I was lost. The house was a maze of hallways and large rooms, all expensively furnished. Whoever this mysterious Roberto was, he was wealthy. He also held all the cards, as far as I was concerned. I would have to wait until this evening to get my answers. I retraced my steps and eventually arrived back at my room.

Now I knew why I hadn't seen the maid in my search of the house. She had been back here. The room had that citrusy, just-been-cleaned smell and the bed was made. On the bed lay a peasant dress and next to it this diary.

Of course, I had hoped that the diary would tell all about my life. No such luck. It was just an empty book. So here I sit trying to fill this empty book with words, hoping that something will jog my memory and I won't need Roberto to answer my questions. I know the truth is in my head somewhere—shining like a lost penny—but I've got to find a way to pluck it from the shadows and let it fall and spin onto the pages of this diary. I can already tell that it's not going to be easy. But, then again, important tasks never are.

There's a knock at the door. Maybe that's Roberto.

It wasn't Roberto.

It was two young women, girls really, armed with baskets of soaps, cosmetics, loofahs and things for the hair. Neither of them spoke English, and both seemed extremely shy. In words I couldn't understand, they ushered me to the bathroom.

For a minute, I watched as they worked in unison, one of them running the bath and laying out big fluffy towels while the other laid out the soaps and lotions they planned to use on me. I was mystified. Was this what rich Mexican women did? Did they have maids who washed them daily? Were they expecting me to take off this robe in front of them and calmly sit naked as a jaybird while they washed me? The answer to that question became clear almost immediately.

They turned to me expectantly. I stood my ground and even though I knew they couldn't understand me, I said, "You can go now. Thank you." They didn't move. They just stared at me as if they were patiently waiting for me to come to my senses. I gestured toward the door. "Thank you. You. Go. I can wash myself," I said loudly while trying to speak as clearly as possible. Of course, this was stupid. It wasn't as if they were hard-of-hearing; they simply didn't speak English. I could yell at the top of my lungs, I could enunciate perfectly and they still wouldn't understand me. So there we stood for probably ten minutes. Me, gesturing for them to leave, and them, smiling and gesturing for me to take off my robe. All the while, that perfumed bath calling me. Okay, so I caved in. When in Rome, right? But I swore as I sunk into that bath that as soon as I was shampooed and scrubbed, these two women were out of here. Famous last words.

I never felt so pampered in all my life. I let them wash my dirty hair in the rose-colored marble bath, let them tilt back my head as they poured cool water over my hair. When they scrubbed me with the loofah mitt, it was like my entire body was being sanded down and polished. By the time I emerged from the tub, I was putty in their hands. I wanted to be taken care of. I wanted to forget that I was a person without an identity.

They smoothed lotion after lotion over my body— all with such sweet smells that I felt transported. My troubles really didn't seem so bad. I let them wax my legs, tweeze my brows, powder my body and apply polish to my nails. Of course, I knew I was probably like the fatted calf being readied for the slaughter. But I didn't care. Not then, anyhow. The last thing I thought as they tucked me into bed for an afternoon siesta was: Whatever my life had been before, whoever I had been, this was something a girl could get used to.

The next thing I knew I was being awakened by the same two young women. How long had I slept? I didn't know. No clocks. But it was dark out. They were gesturing to me again. I couldn't imagine what they wanted this time. I didn't object, I just did as I was told.

I watched as they expertly applied makeup and did my hair. When they finished, they dressed me in a soft cotton dress. I felt beautiful. I looked in the mirror. I was beautiful. And the question came again: Who was the woman who stared back at me? What was important to her? Suddenly, there was an image. Fuzzy, nothing I could make out clearly. A hand slapping me brutally across the face. I pulled myself back. I didn't like what I'd seen. Oh yes, I was sure of it now. There was a lot of pain in my past. Did I want to remember?

Okay, who does this Roberto think he is?

Remember how I said I knew I was probably like the fatted calf being readied for slaughter, but I didn't care? I care now. Here I am sitting in this room waiting for this Roberto guy to come and bring me dinner. He's had his little maids scrub, soften and paint me up, and now he probably thinks he's going to waltz in here tonight and bed me down. Well, I may not know who I am, but I know I'm not easy. I know I'm not going to be pushed around or forced to have sex with anyone.

Whoa. There it is again, another bad image. Fuzzy, just like the last one.

I can't breathe. I feel like I'm being suffocated. Weight on top of me. I can't move. He's holding me down, his smell stinks. He's ripping at my clothes.

Okay, that's it. I don't want to remember this. I can't. I wonder if I can pick and choose what I want to remember and what I don't want to remember. And if I can't, maybe I should just start over. I mean, so far this wasn't such a bad day. Maybe it wouldn't be so bad if today was the first day of my life.

I can't think about remembering any more right now. It's making my head hurt. I'll think about it tomorrow. Besides I've got to think about Roberto and how I'm going to handle him. He's got the upper hand. Let's face it. I'm in his house, eating his food. I don't know how close I am to a main town.

I'm just plain dumb. I should have spent the daylight hours figuring out where I was and how I could get away. Instead, I let myself be lulled into being powdered and pampered. I'm stuck. I'm trapped.

Okay, how am I going to handle this? Well, first of all, I'm going to make it real clear to mister Roberto that I am not some little girl that can be pushed around.

"Don't even think about having sex with me because I am not having sex with you. Let's get that straight right here and now."

That's how I started the evening. Real smooth, huh? The thing is, I was so worked up by the time he got there that I couldn't help myself. You'll remember I decided that I didn't want to think about the past anymore. So, what else did I have to focus on but the future? That's the thing about not having a past. You've got nothing to keep you anchored. Nothing that tells you you're bigger or better or stronger than the circumstance you're in at the moment. You've only got the moment. You don't know how you handled this in the past so you're secretly terrified you can't handle it at all.

Roberto, on the other hand, started the evening much more composed. I heard a soft knock on the door. I boldly walked to the door and threw it open. I was determined to do battle. And there he stood, dressed in a white silk shirt and navy silk pants, a rose in his hand. This rose was all the proof I needed. He was going to try to seduce me. That's when I let him have it. I gave him my strong I'm-not-having-sex-with-you line. Which, incidentally, didn't make me look strong at all. It revealed me to be the frightened, lost soul I felt like.

Then, can you guess what happened next, dear diary? Yes, you got it. He smiled. He smiled that same smile that said he knew what I looked like naked, which, of course, he did. But I don't mean naked as in 'without clothes.' I mean naked as in 'without persona.' You know—that thing that prevents the rest of the world from seeing how vulnerable and worthless we really are. But the knowing smile wasn't the worst of it, it was what he said.

"Good. You don't want to have sex with me and I don't want to have sex with you. Now that we've settled that, perhaps we could go and have some dinner."

That's it, that's what he said, and it was combined with that smile. Then he held out his hand to me and I was so rattled at thoroughly bungling the whole situation that I took his hand and let him lead me to dinner.

Now let's stop right here for a minute. What did I learn? If you're really upset and frightened, don't act like you're really upset and frightened. Act like you're calm and in complete control. I wanted to gain the upper hand in that first moment. Instead I ended up feeling like a child.

Fortunately, the evening went uphill from there. We ate outside in the cool night air. A fireplace roared nearby, keeping us warm. The food was incredible. Flavors of cumin and cayenne. Everything looked and smelled rich and exotic. I still felt like the fatted calf but, once again, I didn't care. Roberto was attentive, charming and sensitive. His sole intention seemed to be making me feel free and secure enough to remember my past.

He let me get comfortable. His conversation was like a good massage—it loosened me up. Then, he gently tried to prod my memory.

"What have you remembered?" he began. Interesting how he said it, don't you think? He didn't ask *if* I had remembered anything, he asked *what*. For a moment, I thought he must really be a mind reader, and I blushed. After all, some of the things I found myself thinking were not the sorts of things I would want him to know.

Yes, it's true. At moments, as I listened to him talk, I wondered what kind of lover he was. I was sure he must be a wonderful lover. His body seemed built for it and he obviously had that talent of making women feel special. Not that I wanted to have sex with him, at least not tonight. He's just the kind of man that makes a woman think about it.

Where was I? Oh, that's right. He asked me what I had remembered. As I said, it was an interesting question, a clever question. Had he asked me if I had remembered anything, I would have lied. I would have denied my flashes of memory. But he hadn't asked me *if*, he asked me *what*.

"I think I remember being abused," I confessed.

He nodded. "Memory is a tricky thing. It can come back in bits and pieces. Sometimes the bits that come back are not the ones we want. People remember things that happened to them when they were six years old, and yet they forget the name of someone they met at a party the week before. It's as though memory is a jewelry box; it has various secret compartments in it where we store lots of different images. Be patient. Other compartments will open. Ones that hold true treasures."

"Why do you know so much about memory?" I asked.

"Let's talk about you." He smiled. And so we did. We talked about me. Or rather, he asked me questions, and I answered. Nothing threatening. He asked me things like, "What's your favorite food?" I answered the best I could. I don't know if the person I was in my past would have answered his questions in the same way, but it was comforting to think that I had favorites. At least it was a beginning.

At the end of the evening, Roberto led me back to my room. Despite his assurances, I still felt unsure of his intentions. Especially when he took my head in his hands at the door. But he merely kissed me on my forehead, the way a father might kiss his little girl.

Did my father ever do that to me? I couldn't help but wonder as I drifted off to sleep. My dreams answered that question. Just not in the way I would have liked.

I saw myself walking somewhere, along the side of a road. The road was surrounded by pine trees. And I was much younger, pretty much a girl, all full of myself the way young girls often are. I watched myself stroll along, my hips swaying, my skirt swinging. I heard my name being called, "Lorelei! Lorelei, it's time for dinner!"

I looked down at my feet as I walked toward a blue and white trailer. I had a feeling of dread. I didn't see him, but I knew he was home. My step-daddy. I knew he'd look at me with that hungry look, that look that made me feel ill. I forced myself awake.

Well, I now knew who I was but I didn't know if I liked the way my life story was headed.

∞

"Lorelei. Lorelei Hills," I told Roberto at breakfast. "It came to me in a dream."

"Good, we have a name." He smiled.

This morning I tried to eat more like a lady. That's another funny thing. Most of my thoughts and actions seem to say I was a tough street-smart kind of woman. Even my skin seems to say I wasn't from the lap of luxury. I mean, if you'd seen my hands and feet before the lotion ladies got hold of me, you'd swear I'd been doing hard labor my whole life. But then, on the other hand, as Roberto pointed out at dinner last night, I seem to know which fork to use. What was I in my past life? Maybe I was someone's maid.

Roberto was staring at me. I felt uncomfortable. I think, in part, I felt uncomfortable because I couldn't read him and I could read anyone. That's why I'm so good at . . . poker.

And there it was; another blurry picture clicked in and out of my mind. I was dealing cards. I felt confident. I felt full of myself. I was a card player.

"What is it? Where did you go?" he asked.

"I just had another memory. I was dealing cards and I was good at it," I said, shaking my head.

"You had a memory. This is good. What is wrong with this?"

"I guess it's just not what I hoped," I replied. "I want more. Something that tells me where I belong."

And I did want more. But not just more as in quantity, I wanted more as in *better*. Let's face it—so far, my past life wasn't exactly a fairy tale. My memories were mainly of abuse. The best I had to say about my life up to this point was that I was a good card player. Whoop-de-doo. Maybe I should be running from my past instead of trying to find it. I needed to change the subject.

"Why is it you speak English so well?"

"I went to New York University." He smiled.

"You did?" I said, wondering if I had ever been to New York City. "Are you from there or from here? From Mexico?"

"I am from here. This very town, this very house. It is my family's estate. It has been passed down from generation to generation."

"Where is everyone now?" I asked.

"They are all dead."

Well, dear diary, I'll tell you when he said that my breath caught in my throat. Red flags went up everywhere. "Danger, danger, Will Robinson!" No family? Wasn't this a culture known for big families? You know, the whole Catholic thing. For the first time it struck me as *off* that he had no wife, no children. He wasn't young. He had to be in his late thirties. I had the strongest urge to get up and run as fast and as far as I could.

He laughed. "I didn't kill them," he said. "I was an only child. My mother died during childbirth. My father died of natural causes five years ago." He paused. "My wife died in an accident. We never had any children." He went silent. In fact, everything went silent. You know that ringing sort of silence, when things go so quiet you feel as if you can hear atoms moving. His face was sad and vulnerable.

I looked at his pain. I felt it. I understood it. Not just in my head—I understood it in the center of my being. I knew, at that moment, that I had lost loved ones, too. I just couldn't remember who they were.

He excused himself. I haven't seen him again today. I don't know if I'll see him tonight.

⤳

It's afternoon. Time for a siesta, only I'm not tired. I'm restless. I've foolishly stayed close to my bedroom all day hoping to see Roberto. For some stupid reason, I want to tell him I'm sorry, sorry I opened up his pain.

People are like minefields. Everything can seem fine on the surface, but you have to be careful where you step. Make a wrong move and BOOM! Pain and suffering flies everywhere. What's that my mama used to say? "It's all fun and games until the crying starts."

Hey—I knew my mother said that. Without think-ing, it just came out. Now I know something else: I called my mother "mama." I heard her voice. And it made me feel good. I couldn't see her clearly, but it was her. I think she was a good person, a good mother. Hallelujah! There's something good in my past.

I want to remember more, but I can't. Something's blocking me. Then, out of the blue, I get that smell. That stink I smelled in my other memory. It's a mixture of cigarettes, alcohol, sweat, dirt and cheap aftershave.

I can't stay in this room anymore. I have to get out and take a walk before it gets dark.

∽

I keep thinking about my mother. Who was she? Could she be missing me now? Could I be a mother? Do I have children out there someplace? If I do, how old are they? Do they miss me?

I examined my body earlier. I was looking for traces of motherhood—stretch marks, enlarged nipples, any-thing that might suggest I'd had a child or at least had a pregnancy.

I have one small, vertical line on my belly. Could it

22

be a stretch mark? Hard to say. I also found lots of scars. Faint ones on my nose and forehead, around my mouth. More apparent ones on my arms and legs. Nothing big, just small wounds inflicted long ago.

What was the cause of these war wounds? Where had my battlefields been? Scars are the body's constellations. If you know what you're looking for, you'll see patterns. Those patterns represent people and events. Wars that will never be won. Lovers that will never be found.

I remember now. I remember a planetarium. I am looking up. The teacher is talking. Telling the story of the stars. Some princess has been kidnapped. A warrior, her lover, is attempting to rescue her. But look how far apart the warrior is from his princess. I feel sadness; he will never rescue her. He will never see her again. For all of eternity, he will be locked in a futile struggle.

The sadness I feel at this moment is overwhelming. Something about this story rings true. Is my warrior out there looking for me? Who has taken me away from him?

Will this loyal love spend his life locked in a futile struggle, too?

I hear Roberto's voice. He is calling my name. "Lorelei." It seems strange to hear my name.

Dinner was very different tonight. I was sad. Roberto was sad. I was sad because of something I can't quite recall, he was sad because of something he recalls too clearly.

I did not ask him about his wife. He did not ask me about my memories. We talked about trees and stars. He talked about his childhood. I talked about my day, no memories included. We drank too much.

We got drunk; a kind of sad-drunk. Not sloppy—at least, I don't think we were sloppy. Just sad. We walked in the moonlight. He took my hand. We stopped by a tree and he showed me where he had carved his name into the trunk as a boy. He held my face in his hands. He kissed me.

He was a wonderful kisser. His lips were soft and moist. It felt like we were one. His tongue slipped into my mouth as he pulled my body to his. Every curve seemed to fit. I could feel his desire pressing into me. I didn't want it to stop. I wanted to stay there forever. We were safe there, our past couldn't touch us. He had no dead wife and I had no lost warrior.

Then a dog barked. We pulled away. The spell was broken.

We looked at each other sadly, both knowing that what we'd felt wasn't a desire for each other as much as a desire to escape. He walked me back to my room. He said goodnight, no kiss on the forehead.

I lie in bed now listening to the quiet of the house. A light breeze blows through the window. Where is Roberto? I wonder. I imagine him sitting in a room, drinking wine, looking at faded pictures of his dead wife.

༄

More dreams. I dream of a mine—a coal mine, I think. It is dark and I am frightened. I smell that stink again. He's not there, but his stink is. I want to get away from this place, but I can't. Every time I take a step to the door, the door gets farther away. I hear my mother crying. I start running and I don't stop. I run so fast the mine can't keep up with me. I am free. I bend over trying to catch my breath. I look up, and he is there: My warrior has found me. He lifts me onto his horse and we ride away. I keep asking him to turn so I can see his face but he won't. Suddenly, I am grabbed from behind. I am pulled from the horse. I am screaming. I am trying to hold on to the horse, trying to get my warrior's attention, but he does not hear me, I cannot hold on. We are separated again, my warrior and me.

I awake with a start. I feel as if I have been under-water. I have to take a deep breath. I turn my head; it is light outside. Good. I don't want to dream anymore.

I dress and wait for Roberto to come and join me for breakfast.

The coffee is getting cold. The juice is getting warm. He does not come.

∽

I wander the house pretending to look for books. I am really looking for Roberto. Don't get me wrong. I'm not looking for him because I feel jilted, but because I just feel lonely. The kiss was good, as I said, but I was not really kissing him. I was kissing some-one I once loved. I don't know who. I wish I could remember.

I find the library. I remember seeing it my first day. I was looking for Roberto that day, too. Only then, I wanted information, and now I want companionship. The library is large and airy. Glass-enclosed bookcases line the walls. There are hundreds of books, all old, all leather-bound and all in Spanish. The only books I find that are written in English are law books. I wonder if Roberto is a lawyer. Strange, I have never asked Roberto what he does for work and he has never offered to tell me. I feel an uneasiness in my belly. I don't know why.

I walk the grounds. It is beautiful here, like a paradise. I come upon a large glittering swimming pool. I touch the water with my hand, it is cool and refreshing. I think about going back to find a maid, ask her to find me a swimsuit, but it seems ridiculous. The place is quiet, and no one is around. I undress and dive into the blue. It feels good underwater. I feel protected. Then, another flash of memory. I am underwater somewhere else and I can't get to the surface. Water is rushing around me, pushing me; I need to get air, I'm drowning. I struggle to the surface both in my memory and in my reality. I have saved myself.

I remember now. A little girl with short blond hair is telling me that if you die in your dreams, you will die in real life. I see myself looking at the little girl. I have blond hair, too. I am ten years old; it is my birthday. I feel terrified that I will die in my dreams. I tell myself that whenever I get into trouble in my dreams I must either wake myself up or change the ending so

I survive. Then the memory is gone. I can remember nothing else.

࿆

I keep thinking about my little blond Yoda, telling me that I must not die in my dreams. I should think that this is silly childhood folklore, but I don't. I dress for dinner and wait for Roberto to come and get me.

I hear a knock on the door. It is not Roberto, it is his maid. She gestures me to come with her. She takes me to the terrace where Roberto and I have had dinner on the two previous nights. Roberto is not there. The table is set for one.

࿆

Dreams. More dreams. Cards are falling from the sky. Jack of Spades, Queen of Diamonds, King of Clubs, Jack of Hearts. Jack of Spades, Queen of Diamonds, King of Clubs, Jack of Hearts. Jack of Spades, Queen of Diamonds, King of Clubs, Jack of Hearts. On and on they keep falling, all the same cards. A child is crying. The cries grow louder and louder. I have to reach this child, but I can't. Jack of Hearts, Jack of Hearts. Gunshots.

The cards are running, the cards are falling. I don't know which card is which, I can only see their blue backs. The child stops crying. Now I am crying and all the while I'm thinking: Don't die in your dream or you'll die in real life.

I wake up feeling like I want to cry. I don't let myself. I never want to cry again.

I get out of bed and shower even though it is still dark. I dress and wait for the maid to bring me breakfast. I do not wait for Roberto. I know he will not come.

I have just finished rereading my diary. I'm getting close to something, I know it. Words and images are swimming around and around in the shadows of my mind, just far enough away that I can't quite make them out. But every once in a while, sunlight catches one of these fishies and for a split second I see their form and color.

I am bored today. I want something to do. I want someone to talk to. I am tired of writing. I am tired of trying to remember.

∾

I saw Roberto today. He did not see me. I was wandering the grounds when I saw him talking to another man. The other man was large and muscular; he looked like one of those bouncers you see at nightclubs.

More images. I am standing in a smoke-filled nightclub, filled with mostly men. They all seem to be drinking or smoking cigars or both. I smile at a man across the room. He is my partner. Lover? Business partner? I don't know. I just know that I am connected to him in some way. I turn and look to another man, and I smile. We are up to something, my business partner and I. I look down at my hands and I begin to deal.

That's it—I remember nothing more. But it's getting better. That little fish stayed in the sunlight for quite a while.

So where was I? Oh, yes. Roberto and the bouncer. I watched them talk. I couldn't hear what they were saying. I'm sure I couldn't have understood them, anyway. Maybe I would have been able to pick up on a word here and there. "Por favor," "uno momento," "la esperanza." Hmm. A little twinge at that last one. Anyhow, back to the point of the story. The bouncer had a gun. He pushed back his jacket to put his hand on his hip and there it was, a black and silver handgun.

All of a sudden, I understood—this guy was Roberto's bodyguard. It wasn't anything they said, obviously; it was what they did. Their body language told everything. Roberto was in charge, he was the boss. The other guy kept nodding his head. Roberto pointed toward the house and then toward the front gates. The man nodded again. Roberto looked closely at the man's face as if to see if his instructions were understood. The two men parted.

So, why does Roberto need a bodyguard? Is it that dangerous in this part of Mexico?

Knock, knock.

"Come in," I say, forgetting that the maid speaks only Spanish.

But it is not the maid. It is Roberto.

◦⌒◦

Roberto apologized. He said that he had business to attend to. He said that that's the reason I haven't seen him in two days. We both know he's lying. Not that he didn't have business; I'm sure he did. But that wasn't the reason he stayed away.

He was back to himself again. He was confident. Master of his universe. He asked me if I would like to go into town for dinner.

&

"You look beautiful," he says as he places his hand on the small of my back and leads me to the car. It is an expensive car, a silver Jaguar, black leather interior. He opens the door, and I slip into the seat.

"Thank you," I respond.

As he walks around the car to the driver's side, I wonder if I should ask him about the bodyguard. I decide I don't want to. I don't want to trip on another landmine.

We are different with one another tonight. We are comfortable but tentative. We know each other now—maybe not everything, but we've seen behind the masks. He knows I can be hurt, I know he has been hurt. And that's where the tentativeness comes in. It is not because we are embarrassed by our kiss the other night, as you might think. It is because we know there are wounds still sensitive to the touch.

The restaurant is the type of place that locals go when they don't feel like cooking. He holds my chair for me. I smile up at him as I sit. We order beer and drink it out of cold glass bottles. He tells me about the town, its history. He tells me more stories of his childhood. I find that I love listening to him. His tone, his accent—it sounds like music to me. He makes me smile and laugh. I like to laugh. I wonder how long it has been since I have really laughed. The food arrives, and it is simple but good.

When we finish dinner, he takes my hand and walks me around the plaza, showing me where he went to school, where he went to church, where he had his first kiss. Everyone knows him here. He waves and smiles at everyone. They smile back at both of us. I am accepted because I am with him.

It is late. He walks me back to his car and we drive home. Neither of us talks about when I will leave, if I will leave. I don't know if I want to leave anymore.

He takes my hand to help me from the car, and he doesn't let go. I don't let go either. He leads me to my room. We say goodnight without a kiss.

I dream only of Roberto.

෴

For the first time since I have been here, I wake up feeling happy. I shower and dress, feeling sure that today will be a good day. I just hope I don't have any memories that will ruin my mood.

There is a knock on the door. I say, "Entra." I am learning. I turn, expecting to see the maid carrying my breakfast. It is not the maid; there is no breakfast. It is Roberto.

"I want to show you something," he says.

"What?" I say, cocking my head to one side.

"The most beautiful place in the world."

I smile and he leads me out the door. Once again he places his hand gently but firmly against the small of my back. We are like old friends; we are like new lovers.

Today we take his Ranger Rover, and I see why. We drive for miles over mountains. Finally, he stops the truck. I don't see anything so different from anything we've seen on the drive here. We get out and Roberto walks to the back of the Range Rover and pulls out a large picnic basket. He takes my hand and leads me down a thin, dirt path. We walk for probably twenty minutes—nothing. Then, all at once, I see it below us, a pool of green water. It looks like an emerald. I've never seen water like it.

We continue down to this incredible jewel and when we get there it is even more beautiful than I first thought. There is a waterfall to one side. At a sunny

34

spot he places the basket on the ground. He looks at me and I can see that he is happy that I like it. For some reason neither of us understand, we start laughing and he picks me up and carries me under the waterfall.

The cold water soaks our clothes. I am wearing white linen and little else. His eyes explore every inch of me. He cannot let go even to preserve my modesty. I want him to see, I want him to know. He closes his eyes, breaking the spell. He sets me down, takes my hand and leads me out of the waterfall. My body is flush with his desire and mine.

We come back to our sunny spot and I lie down and let the sun and warm air dry my body and clothes as Roberto unpacks our lunch. The food is rustic but tasty. Tamales with red chilies and mole, corn and black bean salsa and fried plantains. The wine is young, red and cool. Our lunch is relaxed and unhurried. Perfect. This could be the best day of my life. It's certainly the best day I can remember.

It is dark by the time we arrive home. I know it's strange how I call this home, but I can't remember any other home. It is the only place that is familiar to me. And isn't that what home is—a place that feels more familiar and, therefore, more secure and comfortable than any other place in the world?

We sit on the terrace and eat a light dinner. We drink wine and he tells me about local politics and town gossip. The conversation is at times very serious and at others times very light. There is no uncomfortable silence between us. After dinner, he takes my hand and we dance to the soft melody of Spanish guitar music.

When the music stops, Roberto reaches his hands behind his neck. He unclasps the chain that holds a beautiful silver ring. It is an exquisitely handcrafted filigree design. "This ring has been in my family for many generations. Now it will grace the hands of a beautiful woman." He takes my left hand in his and slips the ring on my finger. It occupies the place meant for the wedding band.

"Roberto, I cannot take this beautiful ring from your family."

"You are my family now, Lorelei. This ring was meant for you."

This time when he takes my face in his hands, he is not drunk. I am not drunk. He looks deeply into my eyes and his soft lips kiss me lightly. It is a romantic kiss. Neither of us is trying to forget anything. We are not running away this time, we are moving forward. He picks me up and carries me to my bedroom.

He parts the netting as he places me gently down on the bed. He stands back and removes his shirt. In the moonlight, I can see his well-defined chest. The hair on his chest is dark. My eyes move down his body.

I want this man, I want to make love to him all night. He parts the netting again and joins me on the bed. He kisses me, lightly at first and then more passionately. His hand is slipping up my skirt, tracing the inside of my thigh. It is a heady experience. We are undressing each other at just the right pace. Not too slow, but not too fast. There is no need to rush; we know we will be here all night. Then, we are both naked. Our bodies move against each other as we kiss. We explore each other. He is on top of me, his weight feels good on me. Everything stops. He looks at me, kisses me and I am filled with him.

We fall asleep in each others' arms. I am dreaming again. I have lost something. No. Someone has taken something from me and I can't get it back. The thief is a woman. Is it the same little blond girl who told me not to die in my dreams? Only now she is all grown-up? I am trying to find what she has taken. I hear gunshots. I tell myself: Don't die in this dream. More gunshots. Only now I am awake. Roberto is telling me to stay down. He pulls me under the bed. I hear him say, "If I'm not back in five minutes, run." I want to ask him where. But nothing comes and he is gone.

He is not back in five minutes. There is the sound of helicopters overhead. People are yelling in Spanish. Sounds of gunfire come from everywhere. I start to run from my room, but my diary, I cannot leave it behind, it is all I have. I am afraid I might forget what I have remembered, that's why I keep writing in it. The next time I get lost I want to have a map to get me home. I grab it up from the bedside table. I am screaming for Roberto. I run to the hall, glass is flying through the air. I see a man, it is the same bodyguard I saw with Roberto. Thank God. He will know where Roberto is.

"Donde está Roberto?" I scream. As he turns his head to look at me, I am hit with a spray of blood and gray matter. He crumbles, I scream and fall to the ground. Blood seems to be everywhere. I look for an exit. I don't know where to go.

I start running and I don't stop. I run so fast that the gunfire can't keep up with me. I am free. I bend over, trying to catch my breath. I look up; he is there. Not my warrior, not Roberto. He is an old man in an old pickup truck. I can see he is horrified by my appearance. He says something in Spanish and ushers me into his truck. I do not resist.

The next thing I remember he is pulling me from the truck and pointing to a water spigot coming from the ground. As I turn to clean my face, I hear his truck pull away.

The water feels good against my skin. I start scrubbing myself and I can't stop. I want to get the blood and tissue off me. I look down at my feet and see the residue of the bodyguard running down a drain. I keep washing. I know I am washing Roberto away as well and I want to pull the cap from the drain and bring him back. I am alone again. Then everything slows down, I feel as though I'm moving underwater. I look to the diary. I know now. I know who I am. It all snaps into place like a puzzle. All at once I have a history.

I have to write it down. I want to save these files before I lose them again. I look around. People are staring. I hadn't realized that I wasn't alone. I look around the plaza.

"Pluma," I yell to no one in particular. They just stare. I start running from person to person. "Pluma? Pluma?" I must write down my life story before it fades again. Maybe my memory is like a dream, maybe it will slowly slip away as time passes, leaving me with nothing but a vague feeling that something happened and I was there. Finally, an old man offers me a pen.

"Gracias," I say. Just a few more minutes and I'll have it all on paper. No one can take it from me, then. I run to a bench and I begin to write.

༄

I was born in Albemarle, Virginia. All I wanted to be was an actress. I would see them on TV on my mama's

39

stories. They were all rich and beautiful and clean. They had pretty dresses and lots of jewelry. Everyone treated them with respect. I wanted to get that attention. I wanted people, especially men, to adore me. I knew I had the looks for it.

By the time I hit thirteen, all the boys would stare at me when they thought I wasn't looking. The men, too. Especially my step-daddy.

I never knew my real daddy. He died in a cave-in in the mines when I was just a baby. He didn't have any life insurance. My mama was in rough shape. She couldn't support me on her own and I guess she figured that any husband was better than none at all. So, when Rayford came along, she married him.

Mama said he was nice enough in the beginning, but I don't remember any of that. I just remember him as mean. He'd get drunk a lot and he was prone to violent fits of rage. That's when he'd beat us the worst. Not that he didn't beat us at other times, too; there was always a good reason for a beating as far as Rayford was concerned.

My only escapes were my mother's stories, as she called them, and Ben Williams. Ben was my best friend. Ben and I did everything together, when we could. Sometimes his mother wouldn't let him play with me. She thought it "peculiar" for a girl and a boy to spend so much time together. "It could only lead to trouble," she'd say. Ben and I played in trees, built forts out of sticks and blankets, and went swimming in an old mine shaft that had filled with water. We laughed all the time. I liked spending time with Ben. We talked a lot. Of course, I didn't tell him about my plans to be a movie star, that was girly stuff. Ben and I didn't talk about girly stuff.

When I couldn't spend time with Ben, if my mama could swing it I'd go to the movies. As I said, I wanted to be like the actresses I saw in the movies. I'd practice talking like them, walking like them. Julie Christie, Jane Fonda, Ann-Margret—I watched them all, and in my bedroom late at night, I imitated them all. I played with my mama's makeup. I had my different looks for my different actresses. Besides Ben, my actresses were my best friends. I couldn't have any girlfriends. Girls wanted to come in the house and play dolls, but I didn't want anyone in my house. Rayford might come home and start beating up on mama and me. Once, I went to a musical that the high school put on—"Annie Get Your Gun." Now that was a show. I loved Annie, a woman with a gun who wasn't taking crap from any man. That's what I wanted to be when I grew up.

The only good thing about Rayford was that he taught me to play cards. And I'll give him credit—the man could play poker. Of course, he didn't teach me poker out of the goodness of his heart, he taught me poker because he wanted someone to practice on. Problem was, I got pretty good at cards. I didn't like to lose to Rayford, and Ray didn't like to lose, period. He got such a look on his face when I started winning on a regular basis. It was a mixture of shock, rage and humiliation. Here he was, a good card player, and here I was, a twelve-year-old girl beating him. The secret was, I could read his face. I knew every card he held in his hand. His face was like a mirror to me. I loved beating Rayford at cards. Getting an extra kick or slap now and then was worth it. The thing I didn't like was how he started taking it out on mama. That's when I started pretending to lose.

He was worse to mama than he was to me. He'd beat her if the dinner was too cold. He'd beat her if the dinner was too warm or too late or too early. He'd beat her because she smiled at the bank teller or because she wasn't friendly enough to his drinking buddies. There was no way that mama could turn without getting a beating. She wore sunglasses so much you would have thought she was the one who wanted to be a movie star.

I don't know how she felt about it, but the thing I hated most was the belt. Rayford would come down on my back with the buckle end of that belt and, wow, would that hurt. It left marks, too. The really demoralizing thing about it was, I couldn't help mama and she couldn't help me. If Ray was on one of his tirades and mama tried to step in, he'd just make the beating all the worse. I once asked mama why we didn't leave. She said, "There's no place to go." Well, of course there were places to go, it's a big world, but she couldn't see that. Rayford had taken the life out of her. He as good as killed her. I haven't seen her in years, so I don't know if he's actually sent her to her grave yet, but he killed her spirit long ago.

I have to stop now. I can't think about it anymore.

I'm sitting in the back of a truck that's carrying chickens. I'm headed north. I've decided to go to Chicago—don't ask me why, I don't know. It's just the place I want to go. Something about it makes me feel warm.

Where'd I leave off? Oh yeah, with Rayford's beatings. You're probably thinking to yourself that Ray couldn't get worse. Wrong, dear diary. At least the beatings I could get used to. The thing I couldn't get used to were the hungry looks he started to give me when I was about thirteen or fourteen. Nothing is worse than a hungry look from a fat, drunk, sweaty step-daddy. That's when I really started staying away from the house. I didn't want to be alone with Rayford.

I wanted to do things at school, like try out for the cheerleading squad. I knew all the cheers, I practiced them in my room late at night. But cheerleading meant short skirts and bare arms. I had too many bruises for that sort of thing. No, I had to stick to the long pants and the long-sleeved shirts. No one could know about Rayford's abuse. He said that if I told anyone, he'd kill mama. He meant it, too.

Ben was still my best friend. We hung out all the time, when he didn't have basketball practice or base-ball practice. His mother wanted him to be involved in everything. She didn't want him to end up working in a coal mine. She wanted him to get out in the world, to make something of himself. I can't fault her there. Ben had potential, too. He was good-looking, smart and athletic as all get-out. All the girls were crazy about him. I guess that's part of the reason the girls weren't so crazy about me. They couldn't understand why someone like Ben hung out with someone like me. Not that I wasn't pretty, but I wasn't exactly girly-looking. I wanted to be, but as I said, I couldn't be. I had too many bruises to be able to wear skirts and spaghetti-strap blouses. Plus, when you've got a step-daddy who's giving you "looks," you don't want to wear anything encouraging, if you know what I mean.

Funny thing is, I think Ben was in love with me. I

don't know why he would have been; there were girls who were a whole lot prettier than I was, girls who flirted with Ben all the time. I guess I just made him laugh. That's what I did best—I made Ben laugh. My one claim to fame.

One day when we were sitting in the woods, just hanging out, he kissed me. It was my first kiss. I was fifteen. It felt great. His tongue went in and out of my mouth, his body pressed into mine. After that, forget it, Ben and I were making out all the time. We'd go to the woods every chance we got, even in the winter. I started to think I might like to marry Ben. Well, that fantasy didn't last very long.

As luck would have it, Sue Ann Kurlin—perfect Sue Ann Kurlin, whose daddy had a horse farm—caught Ben and me in a compromising position. Ben and I were in our usual make-out spot. His lips were on mine, and the hand he'd just slipped under my shirt was cupping my breast. We were lost in each other . . . until we heard, "Ben Williams, what are you doing with trash like that!" It was Sue Ann Kurlin.

Sue Ann Kurlin had made my life hell since we were little girls. She would poke me and tease me because of my raggy clothes. She'd start nasty rumors about me. She even stole my homework once, copied it, and then turned it in as her own. What made someone like her nasty I'll never know. She had everything—parents who loved her, nice clothes, good looks and a big house complete with a swimming pool. You would have thought she'd be so filled with joy that she'd want the whole world to be as happy as she was. Not.

She really got me this time, though. She took my one thing of value; she took Ben away from me. You see, as soon as she saw us, she turned right around and went straight to Ben's mother and told her how she saw Ben and me having sex. His mother hit the roof. No son of hers was going to be stuck marrying a girl like me just because he'd gotten me pregnant. Ben was grounded, forbidden to see me. Sue Ann Kurlin, on the other hand, started spending all her free time at Ben's house. Ben's mother thought Sue Ann would be a good influence. I don't think I ever had another conversation with Ben Williams.

I didn't blame Ben. I knew about his troubles at home and he knew mine. In her own way, his mother was just as bad as Rayford. Understanding didn't ease the pain, it didn't end the loneliness. It didn't stop me from crying into my pillow at night. I don't think I ever quite got over losing Ben.

To make matters worse, the whole town was talking about me like I was some kind of slut. Half the girls in my class would have been mothers by the age of fourteen if their parents hadn't whisked them off for secret abortions. I was still a virgin, and they were calling *me* a slut? The minister even stopped smiling at me. I had no one but mama now.

I had no place to go anymore, no one to spend time with. Rayford was staring at me more and more. I had a feeling that something was about to give.

It did, on my sixteenth birthday. Rayford certainly knew how to time things. Mama had gotten me a cake. Rayford was going to be out late playing poker so mama and I had planned a special celebration. I loved spending time alone with mama. I lived for Rayford's poker nights. He played poker every Friday night because Friday was payday. He stayed out until dawn. Or so we thought.

It was almost ten o'clock. Mama and I were just settling in for our weekly viewing of "Dallas." We heard the sound of the pickup. We were both on edge. This wasn't like Rayford.

I am back there now. I see Rayford's red, drunken face pushing through the door. He is looking at me. He comes and grabs me up by the hair. I can smell the whiskey on his breath.

"Slut!" he yells. Veins are bulging on his forehead and neck. With his free hand, he slaps me hard across the face. He throws me across the room. I fall to the floor and he starts kicking me. Mama is screaming, trying to pull him away. I curl into a ball and cover my face with my arms. Rayford becomes more enraged.

He grabs me by the hair again and starts to pull me across the floor, all the while knocking mama aside, preventing her from rescuing me. He releases me for a minute, long enough to send mama flying across the room. He turns his violence back on me, bends down, pulls me up and starts to punch me in the face. I start to black out. Then, out of nowhere, a fist right to the stomach. I fall into blackness.

When I come to, Rayford is gone and mama is lying next to me crying. "I'm so sorry, I'm so sorry," she is saying. We cry together.

"Let's leave, mama. We can leave tonight." But she is shaking her head. I know it's useless. We've been down this road before. I put her to bed.

As I walk down the hallway to my own bedroom, I think of the baseball bat that's in the hall closet. I have a bad feeling about tonight so I take it with me to bed.

I can't breathe. I feel like I'm being suffocated. Weight on top of me. I can't move. He's holding me down, his smell stinks. His hands are ripping at my nightgown. One hand is clamped over my mouth. The other is grabbing at me, pawing at me. He tears off my underpants and I can feel him fumbling with his belt.

As he shifts his weight to open his pants, my leg comes free and I pull my knee up as fast and as hard as I can. His rancid breath explodes from his mouth with a gasp. He hits me hard with his free hand and grabs me by the throat, choking me. I pull my knee up again and again, connecting both times. This time he lets go long enough for me to scramble free.

I roll out of the bed and grab the bat. He reaches for me again and I swing the bat as hard as I can. I hear dull thud after dull thud as I swing the bat again and again. I stop only because I am exhausted. Rayford lies dead still. There is blood, a lot of it. I reach for his wrist and find his pulse. He is still alive, but for how long, I don't know. Either way, I have to get out of town.

I get dressed and stuff a few changes of clothes into my knapsack. I need money. Today was Ray's payday, today was Ray's poker night. Even though the thought disgusts me, I return to my bedroom and search Ray's pockets. Five hundred dollars. I take two-fifty of it and fold it into my pocket; the other half I hide in the flour jar, with a note for mama: "Get away if you can."

I know Ray won't find the money before mama. Ray doesn't cook and Ray doesn't clean. I slip out the front door, never to return.

Well, my past isn't pretty, but at least I had one. And remember what I said about needing a past because a past tells you how strong you are? Shows you what you're capable of handling? If my past says anything, it says that nothing's going to get me. I'm never going to die in my dreams.

Time to hitch another ride. I'm in Texas. This state makes me nervous. Texas Rangers and all that stuff about how tough they are on crime. A black Mercedes pulls to a stop.

"Where you headed?" he says.

"Chicago."

"I can take you as far as Memphis," he offers. I jump in.

∿

So here I am in another city, on another day, the morning light bleeding in through the blinds of the anonymous room where I have spent the night. This bed feels like a cement floor; why did I waste precious dollars on this room? I would have been better off in the bus station. Maybe this is what the rest of my life will be like: a series of aimless travels to distant places. Panhandling by day to scrounge up enough money for a hot meal and a dry bed. Picking through the Goodwill bin for some decent clothes to wear. Voices heard through the wall, the soundtrack of someone else's life. My own soundtrack has become pretty desolate: The squeak of the springs in whatever inadequate bed I've slept in that night; the shock of cold water from the shower as it runs down my body, jolting me into the uncertainty of a new day.

I'm in a motel in Memphis, trying to remember my life's story. Just as I feared, it has faded, like a dream after waking. I had it all in Mexico, but I couldn't write it down fast enough. I wonder if the memories will come back.

∾

I haven't been in Memphis long enough to get a line on this city. There's so much here, between the landscape and the rib joints and Graceland; it's voluptuous, like a woman, but impenetrable to someone like me— an outsider.

That's what I am, wherever I go. I can hide it pretty well, from everyone but myself. I walk the streets seeing couples strolling, arm in arm. Everyone seems to have someone. Everyone seems to fit, not just into Memphis, or into a couple, but into themselves. But not me.

Not that I feel sorry for myself. I don't have the luxury of sitting around and fretting about what might have been. I'm on a mission to find out what was— the life I lost—and what will be—the new and better life I'll have to create from scratch. Anything is possible—isn't that what they say? Well. If anything truly is possible then I want a life that's real. Where I don't have to be afraid. Where I can laugh and love and be myself, when I've finally figured out who-all that is. . . .

⁊

I'm just about out of money. I want to get back on the road to Chicago but I've got to pick up some fast cash. I can't bring myself to beg anymore, but I'm getting a little nervous about my situation. Then all of a sudden it's there, not a memory so much this time as just a knowing . . . like that "muscle memory" thing they talk about with athletes. I know that all I have to do is walk down a busy street and I'll have all the money I need to move on. "Just scout your mark," I hear the voice say, "then walk toward him and take your fall. When he stops to help you, 'fan and pick' him, brush yourself off, say thank you and get out of there. He'll never know what hit him. Take only the cash, dump the wallet in a trash can and catch the first cab or bus you see. Simple, clean and profitable."

Funny thing, though, I reject that idea almost immediately, even though I know now that I can do it and it would be easy. That's my option of "last resort"—to roll a total stranger. Because there's a more deserving soul right downstairs.

I trot down the stairs to the front desk. There he is, the clerk who's been undressing me in his mind every time I walk through the lobby. He is a scrawny little guy with greasy, slicked-back hair and a pencil-thin mustache. He stuffs his porno rag under the counter when he sees me coming and tries to look busy while I walk through the "lobby."

"This is going to be easy"—this thought seems to come from outside me, like a voice in my ear. I walk right over to him with a big grin and introduce myself.

"I'm bored," I say, planting an elbow on the counter. "Got any playing cards I can borrow?"

He pulls out a beat-up old pack of blue-backed "Tally-Ho's" and asks me if I want to play a little rummy. I say sure, but only if he can "teach" me the game, and tell me all about cards, and show me how to shuffle and such. Pretty soon he's asking me if I want to play a little poker, just for fun. I lose a few hands and tell him I'm getting bored and he takes the bait.

Next thing you know, we're in the manager's office playing real poker. He's betting money, and I'm betting clothes. And I lose a little bit at first, too. I want him "hard" on the hook and in the game for keeps. I'm down to my sheer bra and my jeans, and the "mark" is starting to sweat. That's when I slowly start to take him.

Three hundred dollars later I'm climbing down the fire escape from my room.

He was pretty upset when I left him. I don't want to take a chance that he'll get brave, so I'm taking the back way out. I would have gone right out the front door but I had to come back to get my diary. I couldn't bring it down during the scam, it would have distracted the "mark," but I couldn't leave without it. I just made sure I had another way out. The first rule of the con is know your escape routes.

I feel a little bad about taking the guy the way I did. Fifty dollars into the game he started playing with register money. He's gonna have some explaining to do. But then I remind myself: He asked for it. He knew the risks. You play, you pay.

As I write this I'm sitting on a bus heading north. I didn't want to spend money on the fare, but I needed to skedaddle fast. I'll get out at the next town and hitch a ride, and continue on to Chicago from there. For the first time in a long time I feel like I have a little control over my situation. That was so easy, second nature. I look at my left hand cutting and mixing the Tally-Ho's; I didn't even know I was doing it. I watch in amazement, like it's the disembodied hand of a Vegas dealer—like it's second nature.

Second nature. There's that phrase again, sort of echoing in my mind, making me recall something from another time, another place.

It was a city, but not like Memphis. Not voluptuous and inviting. It was electric. It was pure high-octane energy twenty-four hours a day. There's only one place like that in the world: New York City. The memory is kind of broken up right now. I don't recall how I ended up there or who, if anybody, I first hooked up with. I do have a vague picture of a room in a seedy hotel where you pay cash and you put the bureau against your door when you go to bed at night. I just sit back and close my eyes and feel my hands manipulate the cards and the curtains start to pull back, allowing the memories to flood my mind like the summer afternoon sun.

I remember now. The place was called Night-something. Nighttime? No, I've got it: Nightshade. It was one of those after-hours places in the West forties. I don't remember who tipped me off about the job but I heard it was for a cocktail waitress and it was very good money, all cash. I cleaned myself up as best I could in the washbasin down the hall from my room. I combed out my hair and used what little makeup I

had left to make myself look older and more sophis-
ticated than I felt. It was a long walk to the club, but
I couldn't afford bus fare, much less a cab. Truth is, if
I didn't get this job and start working that day I'd be
sleeping on the street that night.

I took a deep breath and walked through the front
door and down a dim carpeted stairway. I came to another door, but this one was locked. I knocked and a
disembodied voice startled me: "We're closed."

I pressed the intercom button on the wall. "I came
about the waitress job," I yelled into it.

"Hold on." The door opened and I got my first look
at the woman who saved my life.

Her name was Maggie. She was beautiful, or once
was, but hard living had etched deep lines into her
body and face. Whatever pain and suffering she'd had
did not steal the beauty from her eyes, or the kindness
and humor that I could see through those azure blue
windows to her generous soul. She looked me up and
down and said, "Sorry, honey, you gotta be twenty-one
to schlepp booze in this town."

"I am," I protested weakly.

"Sweetie, you got any I.D.?" she asked.

I didn't. My eyes welled up with tears. After all I'd
been through it seemed odd that I'd lose control just
then. I was a survivor; a couple of nights on the street

wouldn't get the best of me. I'd been through tougher times. I guess it was just the loneliness I felt and the goodness I'd seen in Maggie's eyes that had given me a moment's hope—and not just for a job, I suddenly realized. Hope for the love I so desperately needed. Hope for the mother I'd left behind.

I mumbled a thick, half-sobbing thank you as I turned to leave.

"Ah, shit, come on in kid, let me see what I can find for you." I never knew what changed Maggie's mind that day. Maybe she saw in me something like what I saw in her, only from the other side—the daughter she'd never had, or the little girl she never got to be. Whatever led her to take me in that morning, I knew instantly that for the first time in my life I had someone, besides myself, who would protect me.

She brought me inside and the first thing she did was order a big lunch for us. I guess she could see that I hadn't eaten in a while. After she put down the phone she held out her hand and introduced herself. She asked me all the pertinent questions about where I lived—you know the drill. While we waited for our food, she showed me around the club. It looked pretty much like any other nightclub-type place I'd ever seen in the movies or on TV. A long bar, an area with tables and booths, and a large dance floor with one of those mirrored globes hanging in the middle of it.

I wondered aloud why they called this an after-hours place, and Maggie kind of chuckled.

"After hours," she said, "is what goes on in the 'real' Nightshade." And she opened a black door in the black wall; I hadn't even noticed a door was there. It was like a whole other hidden world back there, a parallel universe: a casino. "Members only," Maggie said, and she shut the door.

About the time the food arrived, so did Jackson. He sat at the end of the bar, lit a cigarette and just stared at me, never saying a word. Maggie kept glancing over at him, kind of nervously, but he said nothing. Just kept staring. There was one thing that was obvious about Jackson Benedict: he was the most beautiful man I'd ever seen. He had auburn hair, expensively cut, and an even tan that said he liked to vacation in the sun. His suit was dark and perfectly tailored with a starched, white shirt and a shimmery blue tie. That outfit hung on him like it would have on a mannequin in a fancy department store window. I'd never seen a person look so . . . perfect, I guess.

After a half-hour or so of just sitting there staring, he called to Maggie and she gave me a wink before she turned and walked to the end of the bar. I couldn't hear much of the conversation, only the yelling parts, which didn't sound too promising . . .

"We can't have a minor working in here, Maggie. It's against the law. You know how important it is that everything out front be on the up and up."

"So," Maggie said, "put her where the law don't shine. Put her in the Club Room."

"What?" he said, his voice rising even more. "Back there? Are you crazy? They'll eat her alive."

"No they won't, Jack. We won't let them." Maggie lowered her voice then, but I could still hear what she was saying. "I'm telling you, this girl is special. You know your end of the business, but I know mine. She'll have them eating out of her hands in no time. I promise you."

I was trying to pretend that I wasn't trying to listen, so when he got up and started to walk over to me I just turned my attention to my fried chicken and prayed he wasn't going to throw me out on my ear.

"Lorelei, my name is Jackson Benedict, I own this establishment." He held out his hand for me to shake it. Well, I figured if he was gonna give me the heave-ho at least I'd show him that I wasn't some cowering little girly-girl who couldn't handle herself. I reached out and grabbed his hand and gave it a good squeeze. And, oh God, what a beautiful hand it was—large and strong, but the skin was smooth and clean, and the nails were manicured. I'd never seen a man's hand like that back home.

I guess my handshake surprised him because his eyes widened a little bit and a little smile crossed his lips.

"Maggie tells me you're the 'goods' and that I'd be crazy not to hire you. Well, I'm not crazy and there's no one in this world that I trust more than Maggie, so I guess you're hired."

Something in the way he said this told me not to scream and throw my arms around his neck right then. As nice as this man spoke and looked, I could tell that he was no one to take lightly.

"Thank you, Mr. Benedict, sir," I said.

"Now here are my rules: You come to work in a clean and pressed uniform and you get here at least one-half hour early. Maggie will take you shopping for your uniform. Get three of everything. You wear it once and bring it to the cleaners. The price of the uniforms is an advance against your pay. As far as pay goes, you live on tips here—nothing on the books for Club Room employees. So every week you'll pay a portion of your tips back to me until you've covered the price of the uniforms. You treat all customers with respect. If you have trouble with a customer you bring it to me and I'll handle it. These people pay a lot of money just for the privilege of walking into this room. They expect world-class treatment and they get it here. If you're caught dating a customer, you're fired. This is your warning for any infractions. One mistake and you're gone. That's the way it works here. Do you understand?"

I couldn't even answer, I was so intimidated. Instead I just kind of gulped and nodded. He turned and gave Maggie a hard look and started to walk back to the other end of the bar—but then stopped and turned back to me and asked, "Is that pile of fried chicken bones all from you?"

"Yes sir," I said. I could feel the blush rise in my face.

He turned away again. "Well Maggie," he said, heading for the far end of the bar, "you better get her some dessert before she starts gnawing on your arm."

I watched him walk away, tall and lean, muscular and athletic, yet he glided with every movement. Nothing he did was awkward. It was like watching Fred Astaire in a football player's body. He crossed to the other end of the bar and sat back down. Without any obvious movement he suddenly palmed a cigarette into his mouth and it was lit before I ever saw the lighter. That was the coolest thing I ever saw, at least until I watched him shuffle a deck of cards. But I'll write about that later, diary. I'm about to come to the end of this ride. This looks like a nice rest stop with a promising diner—lots of trucks, which means good food and a good shot at another long ride after dinner.

Maybe I can get a lift with one of those big rigs with the sleeper compartment in back.

⁓

Back to my story. By the way, diary, I was right about that rest stop. Great food and a lengthy ride. So I've got plenty of time to write and remember. I'll even get a few hours sleep. It won't be in the nice sleeper cab I was hoping for, but a warm F-250 pickup beats a cold ditch by the side of the road any day.

Maggie O'Brien took me on my first-ever real-life shopping spree. And boy, did we do some shopping. She took me to all the best stores and everyone knew her. She had expensive tastes. The prices on some of those clothes were more than mama had been allowed to spend on me in a year. I started to worry because I knew that this was coming out of my pay and I hadn't even started working yet.

"Don't worry, honey," Maggie said. "With your looks and personality you'll pay this all off in a couple of months." She'd decided that I needed more than just work clothes, and that kind of worried me, Jackson being so strict and all, but Maggie told me she'd square it with him. I remember thinking that if Maggie could handle a guy like Jackson Benedict, then she'd be a real good person to have as a friend. Boy, was I ever right about that.

Over the course of the next few weeks Maggie showed me the ropes of the bar business. How to take orders and serve properly. How to mix drinks and how to deal with customers of all kinds. That might just be the best education I've ever had. Maggie knew people. She could size anyone up at a glance and she sure knew how to handle all of them. And they always left smiling.

Well, things went along pretty well. I couldn't get enough time with Maggie. She was like having a mama, big sister and best friend all rolled up into one. Even so, as much fun as we had together and as good as she was to me I always had the feeling that she was holding something back. I think Maggie lived a double life. She drove a Mercedes, wore expensive clothes, and had a big, beautiful apartment. She made good money at Nightshade, but not that kind of money.

I went on living in that fleabag hotel for the first couple of months and it probably would have stayed that way for a while had not Jackson seen me coming out of it one day as I was leaving for work. He drove by about three blocks later and offered me a ride. Jackson never said a word to me about having seen me there; I think he knew I would be embarrassed. But, later on that night Maggie confronted me about my room. I called it my "humble commode."

She wasn't surprised by my answer but she clucked her tongue and said she couldn't let me go back there. I would stay with her until I got situated. I'll tell you right here, diary, that I was too happy about that to even pretend to protest. Maggie could see that. I think it made her happy, too. The truth is, dear diary, at that moment I didn't ever want to "get situated." I loved Maggie, right then, like I'd never been able to love anyone before, at least as far as I can remember.

The best times with Maggie were at home in her apartment. I did all the same things with Maggie that I used to do with mama: watching old movies, reading about the stars in the tabloids; but at Maggie's I knew I was safe. No Rayford. No beatings. I don't think I've ever felt so loved and safe. . . .

I just had the strangest feeling, diary—that there was another time when I was loved, a time I felt safer and more complete than any other time in my life, but I can't see it. It's like I can feel it on the other side of a thick curtain but I can't find the opening. It feels so real.

I need to rest a little bit. That was more than merely a feeling I had just then, it was more like a foggy memory. As if I was recalling the events of a past life. This

is making me feel very sad, all of a sudden. I'm going
to try to take a nap.

◦◦

I'm dreaming again. Strong arms are holding me. I
struggle and scream and try to wrench myself free. I
have to get free or they will be gone and I'll lose them
forever. They? They who? I can barely see them
through a foggy haze and they're being led away from
me. I can't make out their features but I know they're
the people who love me. They're looking for me. I
want to scream, but a massive hand is clamped over
my mouth. They can't see me.

"Look this way," I silently scream, as if I could will
them to turn around. "I'm here."

They're gone. The hands release me and when I look
around there is no one there. I am lost and alone.

When I wake up, it is dark.

"How long was I asleep?" I said to the elderly man
behind the wheel.

"You were out for a good four hours, missy. That
sounded like some dream you was havin' there."

"It was," I say softly.

He glanced from the road to me, then back again. "You gonna be all right?" he said.

"Yes, thank you. I'm just fine. It was just a silly old dream."

"Well, I'll be taking the next exit. There's an all-night diner where you can wait out the night. You'll be okay there."

After he pulled into the truck stop, I jumped out, gave him a wave and turned toward the diner. I pulled out my dwindling wad of cash. Five bucks is all I can allow myself per meal. I've got about six hours to sunup, plenty of good writing time.

∽

Diary, as much as that dream kind of freaked me out, I can't help but feel positive about the way things are going. I guess it's that I know I have some control of things now. Money is a little tight here on the road, but as soon as I get to Chicago I know that I'll be able to set myself up very quickly. I know that my luck is going to change. Something good is coming my way, I can feel it. But, on to my memories . . .

As I said, Maggie and I had become fast friends. She looked out for me in so many ways: with the customers, with the other staff; she got me to set some money aside in a bank account—"getaway money," she called it—and she took me shopping. We would spend hours browsing the stores. We'd go to lunch and it would blow her mind every time she watched me eat.

I could eat a ton. My favorite meal was barbecued spare ribs with curly fries and chocolate cake for dessert. Of course, after dessert I always had to have a little salty treat, and pork rinds were just the thing to balance my taste buds after a hearty meal.

The first time Maggie saw that, she busted out laughing. She had the most wonderful laugh. For a smallish woman she had a big old belly laugh. You'd expect a laugh that big to come out of one of those opera-singing ladies, you know the kind, who sort of look like houseboats in evening gowns.

I loved to make Maggie laugh, and I was just about the only person who could make her do it whether she wanted to or not. She especially loved my impersonations. All those years of imitating the actresses in the movies gave me what Rayford always said was a useless talent. I believed him, too, until I heard Maggie laugh at my impression of Bette Davis. And making Maggie happy made me feel good about myself. It was one thing I could give to Maggie that she couldn't give to herself.

One day while we were setting up for the evening,

I was entertaining Maggie with my impression of Scarlett O'Hara and Melanie Longworth from "Gone with the Wind." Right in the middle of my impression, Jackson walked by and he stopped dead and listened to me. That was odd. Because I had been working there almost six months by then and except for the time he gave me a ride to work, he hadn't said two words to me since the day I was hired. Maggie asked Jackson if he didn't think I was a hoot. He just kind of grunted and walked to his office. But he had a strange look on his face.

Jackson Benedict was the most fascinating man I had ever met. I remember walking into that "Club Room" on my first night of work. He stood on a landing that was slightly higher than the rest of the gaming area. His expression was completely unreadable, and his concentration was undiluted. A controlled frenzy permeated the air of the room, held in check only, it seemed, by Jackson's commanding presence.

Each table had its own personality, created by the type of gambler that was attracted to it. The roulette players all seemed a little desperate, helplessly following a tiny silver ball around and around and around to its—far more often than not—disappointing conclusion. At the craps table the players were loud and boisterous, all the time, with every roll of the dice, win or lose.

The blackjack tables were a mixed bag. There were the quiet, studious players, erroneously believing they could count cards from a rack of six decks. And there were the nervous, jumpy players who just couldn't sit still. And there were the friendly players who never got tired of the one-way conversation with the dealer.

But the tables I always watched were the poker tables. High stakes only. You didn't walk in this room to play poker unless you had at least twenty thousand dollars, cash. Credit was not extended to anyone in this establishment. No exceptions. These tables were dead quiet, the stillness broken only by the quiet utterances of the dealer calling cards and bets. These table were all about patience. At this level of play, the untrained eye would see what seemed like six mannequins propped in chairs around the table. But to me it was like a drop of clear water I'd seen under the microscope in sixth grade science class: non-stop action.

Way back, when Rayford was teaching me about cards, he taught me how to spot a "tell," which is sort of a legal way to cheat in poker. You have to pay attention every second, and you have to understand people. They react to every card they get. They try not to, of course; they try to control everything—to keep that perfect poker face intact. But they're only human. It might be in the way they bet; or it might be some small gesture they make when they get the card they need.

It could even be something they can't control, like the widening of their pupils when they fill a straight. Whatever it is, if you pay attention long enough, you'll see a pattern. And every player's got one.

I'd been watching table three off and on for the last hour. The guy with the Stetson and boots—I called him Urban Cowboy—might as well have been waving the flag of Texas over his head. Whenever he drew two cards from the dealer in the opening round of bets, he'd done one of two things: if he was holding a pair and a high card, like an ace, he would check or call; if he was holding three of a kind, he opened or raised. He'd been doing it all night and there was only one guy who had been watching. So, every time Urban Cowboy opened or raised, "Caddyshack"—plaid pants and a golf shirt—would fold his cards. He was paying attention to everyone but himself.

Caddyshack was able to control his betting, but he couldn't keep his right foot still. Every time he was holding strong cards, that heel of his would start tapping up and down like some crazed Morse code operator. If any of the other players had bothered to look up from their cards they would have been tipped off by the way his body shook a little as his foot tapped. These guys were rich, but they were horrible card players.

I was standing there daydreaming about how, if I had a stake of twenty grand, I could walk away from that table with fifty in six hours, tops.

"Something wrong, Lorelei?"

I practically jumped out of my skin when I heard that voice over my left shoulder. I spun around to face my boss. I never even heard him coming.

"Sorry Mr. Benedict," I blurted as I fled over to the bar, my face turning as red as the carpet I was walking on.

&

"You sure are writing up a storm there, lady. What is it, your next bestseller?"

Startled, I looked up to see the tallest, scrawniest old man I've ever seen, standing next to my table. He had to be about six-foot five with legs so skinny they'd look just right holding up the tomato plants in your garden. His feet were about a size forty and lodged in a beat-up old pair of work boots. He was dressed in faded work denims and a moth-eaten yellow sweater. His bald, perfectly round head was topped by a blue baseball cap with a strange insignia, some letters and numbers on the front. And his long nose and floppy old ears gave him a "baby-bird" look that was somehow endearing.

My first thought was that this is a lonely old retiree who is looking for a little conversation with his morning coffee. In an instant I knew that I couldn't be more wrong. The immediate, unmistakable emotion emanating from this man was unconditional love. Not just for me, for every soul he encountered.

He sat down without invitation and I answered, "No it's my diary. I know it sounds strange, but I'm trying to find my past and maybe even my future. Writing seems to help me remember." I couldn't believe that I was hearing myself say those words. I would never expose myself to anyone so carelessly. Where were my "street smarts"? Somehow, though, I felt like it was okay to talk to this man. He was "safe." I could feel it in my heart.

"Wow," he said. "I'm just trying to find my way to Chicago. I think you have a little bit tougher road to travel there, young lady."

I barely heard his last sentence. I basically stopped listening after I heard the word "Chicago."

"You're going all the way to Chicago?" I asked.

"Yeah, I'm attending my last reunion with the guys from my old bomb squadron," he said. "I was a chaplain in the army air corps back in World War II. There's not too many of us left, and I'm getting too old to keep on making long trips, so I'll say my final goodbyes sometime this weekend, then I'll head back to my little shack in the woods."

"Oh," was all I could say.

"Hey, what the heck is wrong with me," he scolded himself. "I never introduced myself. My name is Father John." He stretched his hand across the table.

"Lorelei Hills," I said, taking his hand and giving it a firm squeeze. "You don't look like the priests in my church back home. Where's your black robe and white collar?"

"I don't wear those kind of robes," he said, smiling. "I'm a Dominican Brother. We wear a simple brown robe and hood. Since I'm retired, though, I only wear the robes on official business. The rest of the time"— and here he smiled and spread his arms—"what ya see is what ya get."

I had to laugh. Then, venturing lightly, I said, "You wouldn't be interested in having some company for the ride to Chicago?"

"Wouldn't I? Why, I would be delighted, young lady. As long as you don't mind having your ear talked off by this silly, old fool."

"Father John, as long as you give me some time to sleep and some time to write in my diary, I have two ears and they are at your service."

So we finished our coffee and walked out into the parking lot. I was pretty sure which set of wheels he was driving, from the moment I stepped on the pavement. There was a rusty old Ford Ranger, circa 1985, parked directly opposite the front door of the diner. It had a camper shell on the back, and the rear-end was literally papered over with Christian-slogan bumper stickers: "Honk if you love Jesus," "Smile, God Loves You," and so on. I refrained from comment and headed to the passenger side of the car.

Now if you don't know what a Ford Ranger pickup looks like, I can tell you it's about as small as a vehicle can get and still be called a truck. A man as tall as Father John doesn't get into a car this small, he *puts* it on. He could not possibly have been comfortable driving in that position. His knees were bent and sticking halfway up the steering wheel. His shins bumped up against the bottom of the dashboard every time he moved his feet.

Yet, he showed no discomfort whatsoever. Instead, he just whistled a happy tune and settled into his seat and started to drive as if we were in a Cadillac El Dorado. He just drove right along, humming a lot of the time and talking a blue streak. Every once in a while he'd dip his big, bony hand into a huge box of cheese crackers on the seat next to him and stuff a few into

74

his mouth. That's the only thing I remember seeing him eat during the entire trip.

"What's with the crackers?" I asked. "You've got enough there to feed an army of two-year-olds."

"These?" he asked, holding out a handful. "I'm addicted to these things. Have been ever since a little friend of mine told me about them. Care to hear the story? It's a knee-slapper."

"What the heck," I said. "Go for it."

"Well, it was in a little parish in northern Vermont; that's where I live. I was filling in for a priest who was on vacation. It was a children's mass, and those are my favorite. I gathered the children in the front of the altar and we were all talking about God. I asked a little girl what she thought about God, and she said to me, 'I love Jesus.' At that moment this really bright little boy named Matteo piped in with, 'Wow, I love Cheez-Its, too!' So, I looked at Matteo and said, 'Really? *I* love Cheez-Its, too!' Well, that gave the whole congregation a good belly laugh. And I figured that any food that could get a six-year-old boy that excited was worth investigation. I've been hooked ever since."

He nodded toward the box. "Help yourself. They're terrific."

"No thanks, Father," I said. "But that was a good story. Thanks for the laugh."

"Any time, any time."

"Father John, if you don't mind, I'm going to get some sleep now. I've been up most of the night."

"Go right ahead, Lorelei," he said to me. "I won't be lonely. I always have the Lord to keep me company. We haven't talked yet today and I'm itching to thank him for bringing us together."

I tucked myself into a ball on that front seat and leaned against the door, closing my eyes and letting my thoughts drift, my head resting against the window glass.

Dreaming again. It's vivid and real; I can visualize everything perfectly. I can almost smell and touch things, too, the dream is so lifelike. I am sitting at a felt-topped table and I can feel the familiar, smooth back and crisp edge of a deck of playing cards as they leap and dive, spin and flip, in an exotic ballet choreographed by the hands of a master card-sharp. My hands twitch once and the deck shuffles again and then is laid out on the table before me, arrayed like a fabulous peacock-tail made up of blue swirls and dips.

I look up, expecting to see the appreciative smile of a player in awe of my skill with my hands. But there is no player across from me, only a dark chasm, an expansive, bottomless pit. It is there to make a collection, and somehow I know this. Anxious now, I look down and flip a card: the Queen of Diamonds. I flip the next card: the Queen of Diamonds. And the next, and the next, and then I turn over and fan out the entire deck, and to my surprise and even, for some reason, horror, every card is the same: the Queen of Diamonds. Then the hole begins to pull the cards away from me. One by one they flip up into the air and burst into flame as they get sucked into the hole. I can't save any of them if I try to save them all. Somehow I know the rules of this game. I need only one card to win this hand. One Queen of Diamonds. The card becomes mangled in my fist as I squeeze it with as much force as I can muster. All the other queens are gone now, and the force pulls at my arm, my fingers. I can't keep my fist closed any longer. I clamp my other hand over my closed fist, and now I'm squeezing both hands together, but it's no use. I feel as if both arms are going to be ripped off in pieces, starting with the fingers.

And then I can resist no longer. My hands give way, their strength dissipated against the relentless pull of the darkness. My last queen is ripped from my grasp and suddenly it bursts into flames. It flies into the pit, leaving a smoky trail as the only evidence that the queen ever existed.

I lie prostrate over the game table, sobbing. My tears create dark green stains on the tabletop felt, which coalesce to mark indelibly the exact moment and place of my loss.

I feel myself swimming to wakefulness now, moving away from the dream and back into the real world. "No," I mutter forcefully, my jaw set, my mind made up. "Don't wake up. Go back to the dream and change the ending."

But I can't go back to the dream. I can't change the ending because it has long since been decided, and there isn't a thing in the world I can do about it. I crawl reluctantly out of my haze. I'm not sure I can face the pain of unearthing a memory that has been buried so long, and I am truly frightened.

∾

I sit up in the front seat of Father John's truck and rub my eyes. They are wet, as though I'd been crying for some time. Father John is looking at me with a face etched with concern, and I know that what he is seeing is not a pretty sight. But I also know—or suspect, anyway—that the only reason I'd allowed myself to dream this dream was because some part of me knew Father John would be here when I awoke, and that somehow his calming, loving presence would give me the strength to confront whatever demons awaited me in my memories.

"That was a bad one, Lorelei," he says softly, and it almost seems as though he understands what I'd been going through inside that dream. "Do you want to talk about it?"

"No, Father, not yet. First I have to write it all down. The dream was just the key, you see. The writing opens the door. If I don't open it now I'll lose it and I'm afraid it may never come back."

"Okay, Lorelei. I understand. But when you're ready, just know that I'm here to listen. That was always a big part of my job, the part I was always best at. Listening. But do me one favor, Lorelei, okay?"

"What's that, Father?" I ask as I pull out my diary and pen and blink away the last of my tears.

"Call me 'Father John' or just plain 'John.' Save 'Father' for when you talk to the source."

"Okay, Just Plain John," I say as I settle down into my writing, and he smiles at me. I look out to the scene passing by as we drive. Farmhouses and fields, corn and cows—I let my mind drift back, slipping into the past. Sneaking through the door to glimpse the life that I was yet to fully comprehend or remember.

Then everything slows down. I feel as if I am moving underwater. I look to my diary. It is all coming back to me again, every piece of the puzzle. My history is before me, complete. I must hurry; write as quickly as I can before it fades from view. Before I lose it all again.

❦

I'm back there again, back working at Nightshade. I make very good money, enough to keep me in nice clothes, lots of jewelry and, most importantly, food. I've been eating well, and that's a huge relief. I'm sitting at a booth with Maggie and I have her laughing, as usual. She gets such a kick out of how I enjoy my food. For some reason, a plateful of good food makes me want to dance. When I take a big old bite of pepperoni pizza, I feel like a Pentecostal preacher, ready to jump up and down and shout "Amen," but my mouth is full and I know that wouldn't be polite.

Maggie pretends to look under the table to find where I'm dumping my food. "No woman can eat like you," she says, "and stay so skinny."

"Oh, yes she can," I say. "Because I am a food fur-

80

nace, you see. I am a churnin' urn of burnin' hunger."
I stole that from a song I heard once. A blues tune
with a really good, relentless beat.

Dinner is over now and I'm killing time by practic-
ing my technique and playing solitaire. Shuffle and cut,
deal the card face up with a loud "snap" as it is revealed and dropped in place. A clean, perfect row, another "snap," and down goes the next row. The feeling
is unlike anything else on earth. It is simple and complete and satisfying.

All of a sudden I feel eyes on me. I look up and turn
to see Jackson watching me intently.

"Where did you learn to do that?" he asks.

"My step-father taught me," I tell him. "Playing
cards was the only thing he did well in life. Actually,
cheating at cards is more accurate. He would make me
sit with him and practice on Sundays when the bars
were closed. And that's where I got my education."

"Let me show you how a real 'sharp' does it," says
Jackson, and I eagerly agree.

Over the next couple of hours Jackson has me transfixed, as much by his powerful presence as his exquisite handling of the playing cards. And I'm a quick
study. He shows me a technique and I do it first time,
every time.

He just sits there smiling and shaking his head.
"This is second nature to you, Lorelei," he says. "You

were born to this. I've never seen hands take to the cards the way yours do. They're like a duck to water. Not even my own hands come close. Some day you'll be the best, far better than me, I have to admit."

I feel a warm blush creep into my face, but it's not embarrassment. It's pride, satisfaction—and an infatuation that begins to bloom the moment he tells me I'm the best. It's like the word just lights something up inside me, something that has been long denied: Best.

Best. It's a terrific feeling, a feeling of fulfillment that I've never really known before, and which I've been starved for, without really knowing it, as if that compliment is a big and delicious plate of food set before me.

Well, that night was just a blur for the first few hours. I was so happy. I was in love. I knew that Jackson would never fall for a twenty-year-old country girl like me, but I was happy just the same. Nobody had ever admired me before. Mama had loved me, but this was the first time I had ever known a man's respect.

It was a really busy Saturday night and I remember that we were short-handed. Maggie was home sick with some bug and the bartender had just been fired for taking a little cash from the till. Jackson was doing the work of three people, and that's why he didn't spot it. Table two—the new dealer, Charles—was working with a partner. They must have put together a stake and bought their way into the game. Charles was slowly pushing the money to his man. And they were good, too; oh, they were really good. Nobody in the room was any the wiser. Nobody but me.

I took an order and brought it to Jackson at the bar.

"You've got a tag team working table two," I deadpanned quietly. "Charles is feeding the cards to the guy in the fourth chair. They're taking it slow but they'll walk out with forty thousand before the night is over."

Jackson never even looked up or nodded or anything. He didn't even acknowledge that he'd heard me whatsoever, and for a little while I wasn't sure he had. He just filled my order like I'd said nothing unusual, and began setting up glasses for the next. So I served my drinks and then I spied Jackson talking to a "security man" at the bar as I dropped off some dirty glasses. I went about my business for the next half-hour or so, and everything was going along pretty much as it always did. I did notice, however, that the security presence had quietly doubled since I'd relayed my information.

As I approached the bar with an order, Jackson told me to drop my tray and follow him. We were walking toward table two where "security" had silently converged. Jackson touched Charles on the shoulder and whispered in his ear. Charles looked around the room, lowered his head and stepped back from the table.

"Gentlemen, you'll have a new dealer for the rest of the evening. This is Lorelei Hills."

The players all nodded and I sat down. Charles was escorted out a side door by two of the men as Jackson bent down and whispered in the ear of player four. He was already white as a sheet, and he just swallowed hard and nodded. Jackson nodded to me and left by that same side door. I knew exactly what he wanted me to do. And I knew that I could. I was better than any of these rich, sloppy drunks. I would slowly feed them back their money and they would never be the wiser. They'd all go home tonight happy winners, courtesy of Lorelei Hills and chair number four.

The plan went off without a hitch. I sat in my dealer's chair that first night and it felt like I had been there all my life. Occasionally I would glance up at Jackson watching from across the room. He would nod and give me that quick little smile of his. I would nod and quickly go back to my task. I didn't want the players thinking that something was amiss, and I could not afford the loss of concentration that Jackson's smile caused. My buddy Roger was standing behind number four, watching. Always looking out for me, always keeping an eagle-eye on me. He caught my eye and gave me a wink. I looked across the table. *The bet is $1000.00 to you, number four . . . Number four folds . . .*

I know that a real change has taken place tonight. I have assumed a new stature among my peers. In the course of one night I have become Jackson's protégé, and he my Svengali.

The night is over now and I'm sitting at the bar having a drink with Roger. Jackson comes over and sits down next to me. Roger says goodnight, gives me a peck on the cheek and leaves us alone in the room.

"That was good work you did tonight, Lorelei," Jackson says. "Amazing, in fact. Those guys were pros and yet you nailed them."

"They weren't that good, Jackson," I demurred. "You would have caught them yourself if you hadn't been under the gun."

"But I didn't, and they were good enough that Roger didn't spot them, either. You took care of me tonight, Lorelei. If those bastards had succeeded, word would have been out on the street within a week and we would have been out of business. You saved the job of everyone in here tonight. And they all know it." He took my hand and placed a thick envelope into it.

"Jackson, this isn't necessary, I was just doing my job," I tried.

"That's the standard reward for anyone who catches a cheat in my place of business. No special treatment. I run a clean house and this is how I keep it that way. The special treatment is yet to come," he said behind that heart-stopping smile. "Get your things and change out of your uniform. The night is over and now I am going to take you out for a beautiful dinner."

"Jackson, it's five-thirty in the morning," I protested. "Where are we going to find that kind of meal at this time of day?"

With that, he flashed his incredible smile again. This time he wants it to be enigmatic, but he completely fails. It's just beautiful, that's what it is. I feel a tingling sensation rush up from my center and spread out to engulf my entire body.

Jackson's limousine pulls up in front of this shimmering high-rise overlooking New York harbor. We take the elevator to the thirty-seventh floor. The elevator doors open, not onto a hallway with a row of doors, but rather onto a marble foyer with a little sitting area. At the other end is a door, the only one. This must be a very exclusive restaurant. I'm glad I wore my favorite outfit, a short black skirt, high heels and a red, fitted, spaghetti-strap top. Jackson leads me across the foyer. I am open-mouthed in awe of the glamor and luxury of this room. He opens the door and leads me in.

"Oh, my," is all I can utter as I stand there with my hand across my chest.

"Welcome to my 'humble commode,' Lorelei Hills," he chuckles.

I look at him in wide-eyed surprise. For one split-second I have a stab of fear that he is ridiculing me the way so many have done in the past. But when I look in his face, all I can see is gentle, affectionate teasing. I could get used to this.

"All right Mr. Smart Guy," I say when I've recovered. "Nice crib you've got here, but where's my fancy dinner?"

Jackson takes my hand and leads me through his penthouse suite. Everything is tastefully decorated in a contemporary style, with black and white the predominant colors. Obviously the apartment was decorated by a very capable and knowledgeable professional.

"Jackson, this is spectacular, did you decorate this yourself?" I ask innocently.

"Absolutely not, Lorelei Hills," he laughs. "You know me better than that. I am the best at what I do, bar none. For everything else, I find the best in their field and I pay them to do it for me."

With that, he opens a pair of pocket doors into an exquisite dining room. There I see chairs and a burnished ebony table set for dinner. The dining room opens onto a balcony overlooking the harbor. The soft glow of the candlelit room gives way to the dawning of a warm spring morning and is punctuated by the brilliant orange of the rising sun as it reflects off the

Statue of Liberty. My breath is completely taken. I gasp at the beauty of it all.

A waiter discreetly appears to announce dinner, and if he feels the strangeness of this morning meal, he doesn't let on. Once again, I am taken aback at the splendid imagination of Jackson Benedict. Ever the gentleman, he escorts me to my seat and pulls out my chair. After he's seated, the waiter, by some feat of clairvoyance, arrives to pour champagne. Jackson raises his glass to me. As I raise my own glass Jackson says, "To Lorelei Hills, my own personal savior." I say nothing. I just blush, and with an appreciative smile I touch my glass to his, the gentle "ping" of the crystal sounding the depths of my feeling for this man.

I am brimming with anticipation over the beautiful dinner to come. At the same time I am more than a little nervous about which fork I should use. I fervently wish someone had taught me these things, or sent me to etiquette school, or *something.*

"God, please don't let me embarrass myself in front of Jackson tonight," I silently pray. At that moment the waiter appears with dinner and my fears are carried out over the water on the notes of my delighted laughter.

He has placed before me a heaping plate of . . . barbecued spare ribs and spiced curly fries! As the waiter leaves I reach over to punch Jackson in the arm.

"You knew I was nervous about eating fancy food,

and you just let me sit there and stew, didn't you, you brat."

He tries to answer but he can't because he's laughing so hard. Finally, he's able to breathe again and he says, "I've seen how you eat this stuff, Lorelei. If I was going have to sit through that show tonight I at least wanted to have a little fun with it."

"Well, thanks a lot," I say.

"Lorelei, are you disappointed with me that I didn't get a fancy dinner for you tonight?" he asks me as his mood grows quiet. "Because I just thought you would feel more . . ."

But before he can finish his sentence I am up out of my chair and standing next to him. I bend down and wrap my arms around his shoulder. "Jackson, what you did for me tonight was the kindest, most considerate thing any man has ever done for me. I love it and I love you."

The words simply come out of me before I can censor them.

As soon as I've spoken, I am completely frozen with anxiety. How could I have said those things now? Never mind that they're true; how could I have let this beautiful moment be crushed by a silly impulse?

It's too late. There's nothing I can do to take my words back. What's done is done. I feel sick inside, and I slowly return to my seat. No longer hungry, I turn my attention to the food in front of me, hoping he won't throw me out on my ear.

Jackson has not said a word. He's just staring at me intently. He gets up slowly, and I can feel the sobs trying to push their way out of my chest. Please don't cry, I tell myself. Don't lose his respect, too.

He slowly walks to my side. He takes my face in his strong, supple hands and in a calm voice he asks, "How long have you felt this way, Lorelei?"

I can't speak. I am fighting to hold back the tears.

He kisses me tenderly and asks again, "How long?"

I am confused now. Why is he torturing me? I long for his kiss again, all the while knowing the loss will be greater still for having it.

Finally, I muster the courage to answer. "Since the first day I met you," I admit to him.

"Then, Lorelei, you have me at a loss. I have only been in love with you for the last ten hours."

At first I don't understand, and then it suddenly dawns on me. I leap into his arms and he catches me and holds me tightly without any effort at all. He offers his lips to me and, as I kiss him, waves of passion rush out of me, eager to dance upon the shores of this man's heart.

"Jackson?" I say.

"What now, Lorelei Hills?"

"Can we eat? I'm starving."

"Absolutely," he says, releasing me, and releasing a laugh as well. "Let's dig in."

As I take my first bite, the waiter enters the room with a confused look on his face. "Mr. Benedict, sir, did you say I should serve the pork rinds *after* dessert?"

I am standing in the bedroom with Jackson. It is daytime so there is no darkness to hide my uncertainty. I am very inexperienced, even for my young age, and I want so to please him. He does not hurry. He removes his shirt and steps toward me. We remove my clothes slowly, sensually, and I don't feel awkward. I realize that lovemaking can have many stages; that every movement is meant to be a stimulus, an erotic act unto itself. And so, as he brings me to him, my tingling body attentively awaits his caress. He picks me up and carries me to the bed, laying me down with exquisite care. Our bodies entwine and I accept him into me without hesitation. We move together in unison, mutual exploration and shared satisfaction our only destination. Loving Jackson comes easily to me, without confusion or regret. Second nature.

I wake to the sound of piano notes wafting through the air. Jackson is not in bed with me. The clock on the night table says three o'clock in the afternoon. It's Sunday and Nightshade is closed. We have the rest of the day to be together. There is a luxurious white terrycloth robe resting on the bed at my feet. By the size I know it is meant for me.

I slip out of bed and into the robe and begin my search for my newfound love. I follow the sound of the music. Jackson must be listening to the stereo in the living room. The music is beautiful. I'm wondering what artist it is, and thinking that I'd like to get the CD, when I turn a corner and stop dead in my tracks. The music I'm hearing comes not from the stereo but from Jackson's beautiful hands. They are waltzing across the keyboard of an ebony baby grand piano. Jackson looks up just then and sees my open-mouthed awe and he smiles.

"Why so surprised?" he asks.

"You never told me," I reply.

Jackson stops playing and pulls me to him. To my surprise he does not kiss me; instead he puts his right hand flat up against my left. My hand is a smaller version of his: long supple fingers emanating from a wide palm. "People like us have hands built perfectly for two things Lorelei, dealing cards and playing piano. Actually three things, but we'll talk about that a little later. Let's go to the kitchen and have a bite to eat." He gets up and, still holding my hand, proceeds to lead me to the kitchen. I follow him, still thinking about that last statement. What's the third skill my hands were made for?

After "breakfast" we make love again and, like the first time, it's wonderful. We shower together and dress and soon it's after six. Jackson proposes going out for a quiet drink and a late dinner.

I am a little surprised that we don't end up at one of his regular haunts. The bar we come to is off Fourteenth Street on the west side. Just a neighborhood gin mill where the average Joe stops in for a short beer after work. The bartender and patrons all seem to know Jackson and mutter or wave their quiet hellos. I'm sitting in this booth looking over at Jackson and I am more curious than ever.

"Come here often?" I ask, trying to be cute.

"Not as often as I'd like to, that's for sure."

"I just wouldn't have pictured you hanging out in a place like this."

"I don't hang out here, Lorelei, I own the place. It

loses money every year but I don't own it for the profit."

I want to ask him why but I don't feel that one wonderful night together entitles me to know his business. When I don't ask, he continues. "People in bars like this usually have one thing in common. They see everything and say nothing. What I want to talk to you about tonight is sensitive. And before I start, I want you to know that I love you and whatever you choose will not change how I feel about you one iota. Okay?"

"Okay, Jack. Shoot."

"Lorelei, have you ever heard the terms 'grifting,' or 'playing the con'?"

"Sure, it's like phone scams and three card monte and such, right?"

"That and other things . . . bigger things. It's what I did from the time I was sixteen until just about five years ago. I did it all; I learned from the best. I cut my teeth as a 'dip'—that's a pickpocket—moved up to the small con and did pretty well for a guy my age. In my late twenties I hit the big time. My 'crew' was so good. We skimmed millions from huge corporations and governments. Some of them still haven't figured out where the money went. I put away enough to invest in a gaming parlor and spend the rest of my working life doing what I love best . . . playing poker."

I really wasn't sure where he was going with this,

so I ventured a guess. "Jackson, I don't care about what you've done in your past. All I care about is our future together."

"That's just it, Lorelei. I was out, now I have to get back in. I have no choice. And I need your help."

It took me a few minutes to understand what he was asking me to do, and all of the ramifications of the choices I would make. "Jackson, an illegal gambling parlor is one thing. Victimizing unsuspecting people is another thing entirely. I just don't think I could be involved in something like that." I paused, took a deep breath and forced myself to say it. "And I don't think I could be with you if you did."

I think I surprised Jackson because he was quiet for quite a while. But I couldn't tell what he was thinking; his poker face was flawless. His face broke into that wonderful grin, but it was tinged with some regret. "First of all, Lorelei, I want you to know that I didn't victimize innocent people. I preyed on the illegal money-laundering operations of corporations and governments—not ours, by the way. Secondly, if I don't get back in for one more con I'm going to lose everything."

Jackson went on to explain to me how he sank everything he had into Nightshade. Things had been going along beautifully for five years, and then three months ago, it all began to change. There had been a powerful state politician in the club and he had lost a bundle. Jackson suspected that it was money "borrowed" from the campaign fund. He had to recoup those losses before an audit triggered a scandal that would derail his career.

"He can't come at me directly," Jackson said, "because I have security tapes that show him betting in the club. If I get burned, then those tapes go into evidence and he'll be ruined. So he has to pressure me through his political connections. We haven't been raided yet, but that will happen as soon as he can figure out how to bury the tapes. Right now the cops are just harassing our clients. Next they'll start arresting them, for public embarrassment purposes only. They have to catch them in the act of gambling for the charges to stick. So we have some time—three, maybe four months—before the hammer comes down."

I was feeling less uncomfortable about things now that Jackson had explained himself. In fact, I couldn't blame him one bit for what he was planning to do. The only thing I didn't understand was . . .

"Why do you need me," I asked. "I'm completely green at this."

"I need you, Lorelei, because you're good. Look, my crew disbanded years ago. Most are long gone—retired or in jail. I still have my two best people available but I need one more. I need someone smart, streetwise.

Someone who I can trust with my life. One more thing: he has never seen you before. He knows the rest of us. You are the one who can get close. What do you say, in or out? No pressure."

I have to admit I was getting excited about the idea. I've always been a bit of a risk-taker and this was a cause I was beginning to think I could get behind.

"I'm in." I smiled. It was only after Jackson let out a big sigh of relief that I realized he had been holding his breath.

"Thank you," he said. "We meet here at two P.M. sharp tomorrow. Wear jeans, a sweatshirt, dark glasses and a baseball cap. When you get here, the bartender will show you to the back room. That's it. You clear?"

I nodded.

"All right," he said, placing both hands flat on the table, "let's get out of this hole and go eat a nice dinner. Oh, and by the way," and he was standing now, "I was wondering if you would consider moving in with me, starting tonight?"

I walked into the bar at two the next afternoon. Neil, a good-looking fella with dark blond hair and serious eyes, showed me into the back room. Seated at the table were Jackson and the rest of the "crew." Maggie and Roger looked up from their beers and smiled, amused that for once they had caught me off guard.

"This world is getting smaller and smaller," I muttered as I slid into a chair and poured a beer.

Jackson opened the meeting. "Okay, folks, this will be short and sweet. First, Lorelei, as of today you are off the table. I don't even want to see you near the club. I want to make sure you remain anonymous, and anyway, your dance card is going to be full with your lessons. You've got a lot to learn in a little bit of time. And you have to learn from the bottom up. Roger, you'll work with Lorelei on phone technique and designing escape routes. I want you to teach her the bank examiner routine and the bail bond scam. Maggie, you run her through the 'pigeon drop,' get her up to speed on wardrobe, disguise and scouting the mark. I'll run her through picking pockets and the Eliza Doolittle program. And remember, she has to run all these skills successfully before she's ready."

Jackson looked over at me after finishing his instructions. "Lorelei, after you've finished your crash course at the Jackson Benedict Charm School you'll be the fourth best con in this room and you'll be able to mix with Boston bluebloods, bowling alley queens and all points in between. You'll be able to walk into a shopping mall in your underwear and walk out in fur. All skills that I hope you'll never have to use." He turned to Maggie and Roger. "Any questions? Good. I'll see you at the shop tonight."

They nodded and quietly got up and left through different exits.

Then Jackson turned to me.

"Lorelei," he said. "Before you leave there's one more thing I wanted to say. As odd as it may seem, we have a sort of code of ethics in our crew. It's important that you understand this because it will help you make sense of the choices you'll be taught to make in the next few weeks. This is it in a nutshell: Never take money from someone who can't afford to lose it. Don't take from the weak. Know the difference between a victim and a willing participant, and seek to do business only with the latter. Resort to theft only when no other opportunities exist. If that doesn't make sense to you right now, I hope the lessons of the next few weeks will make it clearer to you. Now, it's time to take off. I'm headed to the club. I'll see you in the morning."

Jackson got up and bent to give me a quick kiss before he silently slid out the front door. I put on my cap and glasses and nodded to Neil on the way out of the saloon.

My memory is starting to fade again, diary. There's just so much to recapture. I seem able to grasp only sections. Then I write them down so I have something to jog my recall. I'm hoping someday I'll learn it all and I'll be able to keep it in my mind, so I'll have found myself again and not have to rely on a "history book" for my life's story.

The weeks following the meeting are a blur of lessons in speech, dialects, picking pockets and which fork to use for the salad. And, of course, there were the days and nights with Jackson. I was in love and happy for the first time in my life—or the life that I can recall, anyway. We packed so much into those three months that it might as well have been ten years.

Another thing: I'm sure I was pregnant. I see Jackson's long supple fingers caressing my belly. He still loves me and I am relieved, overjoyed. But I sense darkness again, too. Gunshots and screams. The player in chair number four. Jackson is down. Maggie in a pool of blood. Roger pushing me through a doorway. I am running down a dark alley. I recognize it. I am running so fast the bullets can't keep up with me. I scream for help. I put my hand to my side, liquid warmth . . . a hand full of blood. I am screaming now but not for me . . . for my baby. I collapse on the street. I see a long, black car. The door opens and I am being lifted by strong arms. I am begging for my baby's life. I recognize the long blond hair, the blue eyes. The last memory I have is being put in the car. It's driving very fast. Then, bright lights and voices, faces with green hats and masks. Now the screen is blank and I am so tired. . . .

A dream recurs. Cards are falling from the sky. Jack of Spades, Queen of Diamonds, King of Clubs, Jack of Hearts. Jack of Spades, Queen of Diamonds, King of Clubs, Jack of Hearts. On and on they keep falling, all the same cards. A child is crying. The cries grow louder. I have to reach this child but I can't. Jack of Hearts, Jack of Hearts. Gunshots. The cards are running, the cards are falling. I don't know which card is which, I can only see their blue backs. The child stops crying. Now I am crying and all the while I'm thinking: Don't die in your dreams or you'll die in real life.

❧

"That was another bad one, I think, Lorelei. Is there anything I can do?"

"Yes, Father John. Tell me why God lets bad things happen to people."

He stared through the windshield. The inside of our truck was quiet except for the insistent rush of the oncoming traffic.

"Lorelei, did you ever hear the story about the old man and woman stuck in a flood?"

"No, but don't tell me if it's gonna be sad. I'm fed up with sad stories."

Father John turned and bathed me in the warmth of his baby-bird smile. Then he turned back and continued. "There was this old farm couple in the Midwest. They had worked their farm together all their lives and raised a family. They were people of devout faith. They prayed each day and put their lives in God's hands and things worked out pretty well for most of their lives.

"Then one spring," he went on, "there were torrential rains and a catastrophic flood. The town had been evacuated. The rescue squad came to their house in a truck to take them away. But they refused to go. 'God will provide,' they reasoned. The next day the waters had risen even higher and they were now stranded on the second floor of their house. Again, the rescue squad came by, this time in a boat. Again they refused, saying, 'God will provide.' On the third day the waters had risen even higher. They were now stranded on their roof. The rescue squad came once more to their aid, this time in a helicopter. These were people of deeply imbedded faith in God, and despite their fears they refused once more, saying, 'God will provide.'

Well, not long after that, the flood waters swelled to record heights. The old couples' house was swept away and they were never seen again on this earth. As they were entering the kingdom of heaven they had their audience with God and the old woman couldn't help but ask, 'God, after all the years of faith and prayer, why did you not provide for us in the end?' God replied in exasperation, 'I sent you a truck, a boat and a helicopter. What more did you want me to do?' "

Despite myself I started laughing. Something about the old monk left me feeling loved.

"Now," he said, "some people will say that the moral of this story is 'God helps those who help themselves.' Personally, Lorelei, I believe that it's God's way of telling us, 'The lifeline is always there, taking hold of it is up to you.' "

I smiled. "Good story, Father John. It cheered me up a little bit. But, I disagree. If there is a God, he *only* helps those who help themselves. The truth is I've never seen evidence in the life I can remember that there's a God out there who loves me. I just don't believe in God."

"But he believes in you, Lorelei. God is always ready to take you into his loving embrace. It is never too late to let God back into your life. It is never too late to change."

Though I never said much to him about my life, I could swear he was referring directly to my checkered past. Was he just guessing? Did he spot a "tell"? I guess he figured he'd done enough talking, and we both retreated into our thoughts. After a while we entered the city limits of Chicago.

"Where would you like me to let you off, Lorelei? Do you have a place to stay?"

"Yes Father John. I do. But drop me off at Marshall Field's. I need to pick up a few things."

The battered old Ford Ranger pulled up in front of the Marshall Field's department store on State Street. I gave old Father John a hug and a kiss and thanked him for the ride. He hugged me for a long time. I believe now that he was trying to leave as much love with me as he could before I left. Sort of like the bear getting fat before the long winter nap. He was leaving me with a reserve of love to help me face the trials that, we both sensed, lay in my imminent future.

As I turned to climb out of the truck he said, "Smile, Lorelei. Cheez-Its loves you."

"So long, Just Plain John."

I smiled, gave him a wink and shut the door. As the little blue truck pulled away, the last thing I saw before he turned the corner was a bumper sticker. "Sometimes the answer is no," it said.

Chicago. When Father John's truck turned the corner, I turned to Marshall Field's. I've heard about this store. Upper crust, expensive. People with money shop here. People who think they're safe within the confines of those walls. Thanks for the good thoughts, Father John, but good intentions aren't going to put food in my belly or my head on a pillow. I need a stake. Starter money. Just enough to get some decent clothes, a cheap room and a hot meal.

It's still warm in Chicago. Indian summer has not lost its grip. But I feel a chill in the breeze that foretells a change in the weather. Time to get to work. As I start toward the entrance I spot the doorman giving me a hard look. He gestures and I know I won't get two steps in through the door before security is all over me. In the guise of being helpful they will hustle me out of the store as quickly and quietly as they can. I look at my reflection in the glass. I'm like a neon sign. They know what I am, they know why I'm here. But, they don't know what I know.

I don't go through that door. Not only would it be fruitless, it would sour the place for me. If I went through that door they would get rid of me, then they would alert the guards at every entrance. This guy has got me pegged, I'll never get in any door he's in front of. But, there are always other doors.

I pretend I'm peering through the windows in search of something. I don't see it. I turn and walk to the doorman.

"Excuse me, sir."

He looks up with suspicion.

"Could you please direct me to a pay phone?"

After a moment, he points to a corner a couple of blocks down the street and grunts some unintelligible directions. I say a respectful "thank you" and I turn directly and head to the pharmacy on that corner. I don't look back or hesitate. I'm smiling because I know he took the bait and he has signaled the all-clear to his back-up. I don't have to see him do this to know it's happening. I know. Second nature.

I enter the drugstore and browse for about five minutes. They are watching me in there as well. I don't go around any corners out of their line of sight, I keep my hands in plain sight and I don't touch anything. Finally, I walk to the counter and buy a pack of gum.

When I leave the pharmacy I turn and walk directly away from Field's. I don't even glance in that direction. He has probably forgotten me by now, but I take no chances. I always hedge my bets.

I have wandered around the streets now for about two hours. I want to make sure they have lost the scent. Always careful. Finally, I can move closer. I spot up on a corner at a bus stop and post my watch. Fifteen minutes, half-an-hour. There he is. I've got my mark. He's dressed in expensive clothes, he's alone, and he's carrying three shopping bags. I almost burst out laughing when I see him stop outside the store and reach into his left breast pocket and pull out a tip for the doorman.

"Geez, why don't you just walk over here and give me the money?" I'm thinking.

He picks up his bags and starts walking down the street to the corner opposite me. The set-up is a little tricky because if the traffic light goes against me, I'll have to jaywalk to get to him. That calls attention to me. If I don't get the light, I'll bail on this one and he'll go home none-the-wiser of his near-miss. But the grifter gods are with me this fine autumn day. I start crossing the street with the light. I feel like an air traffic controller tracking two blips on the radar screen. Only, in this case, a collision is a good thing, for me anyway.

I'm staring straight ahead as I converge on my prey. He actually turns toward me at the corner just as I kick my toe into the curb feigning a trip. I fall right into him and he catches me. I mumble a "Sorry" and an embarrassed "Yes, I'm fine" and I'm on my way. Five seconds tops, probably three. Second nature.

I zigzag streets for a few blocks and spot a Mc-Donald's. I duck into the ladies' room and enter a stall. A little over four hundred bucks. Not bad. Enough to get me some decent clothes and a cheap room. I drop the billfold in the trash as I leave the rest room. I wander until I find a discount clothing store. Two hours later I'm holding a bulging bag and hailing a cab. This is the only cab ride I'll buy for a while. I hate the cost but a cabbie will have the information I need.

This room is disgusting but at least it's cheap. I have enough left over for a couple nights' stay and a few cheap meals. And the hot water works, so I can take a real shower. It's been a long time. I look around the dreary room and I'm feeling anxious for some reason. Something about the memory of that man's face as I lifted his wallet. He was startled but then concerned. He really seemed to care that I was okay. I guess I'm feeling guilty. Last resort—isn't that the rule, Jackson? The sound of his name in my mind pulls me further down into the gloom. I decide to take a long walk. There's still a lot of daylight left so out I go.

I've been walking for a long time, just taking in the sights. They weren't lying when they said this city is windy. I turn one more corner and a block away I'm staring at a sandy beach and endless blue water. A city with a beach, how cool.

I take off my shoes and socks and walk out onto the sand. There's a pretty little girl playing in the sand while her mother watches. The woman seems serene as she coos into a bundle she's holding in her arms. I can't help but walk toward this little family scene. I feel as if I have to see the baby for myself. But before I can reach them, the little girl runs up to me.

"Will you play sand castles with me?" she says.

For a moment I can't answer her. I'm transfixed by her beauty. Strawberry blond hair that's naturally curly. Her baby-powder complexion glows with cheeks made rosy by the autumn breeze. I cannot look away from those cornflower blue eyes. And I cannot answer her, either.

"Elizabeth, stop bothering the nice lady," I hear from the bench. The sound of that name flips a switch in my mind. My hand travels down to my belly, gently caressing the scar that lies under my blouse.

"Your children are beautiful," I manage to say. "You must be so happy."

"Thank you," she says. "How about you? Any children?"

"Yes, I—uh, no," I stumble. I can't look at her; I have to get away. My face is burning with shame, my mind clouding with confusion.

I am a childless woman . . . or am I? I'm feeling the same sensation I felt in Mexico. Only this time I think I know the reason. New York. Jackson's son or daughter. But why do I feel the sensation so strongly here, a thousand miles away? I have got to get back to my room, to my diary. The diary has the answers. I'm desperate to get back to my room. I hail a cab.

I enter my room and collapse on the bed, emotionally depleted and physically exhausted. I don't want to think about babies or Jackson or Roberto anymore. I just want to sleep.

The dreams come. I'm looking down into a crib at a baby girl. She is dressed in a pink outfit and she is lying on her back, arms and legs flailing. There's a mobile hanging over her—little black and white panda bears on pillows—and she is staring up and laughing as if it's the funniest thing she's ever seen.

She is certainly the most beautiful thing I have ever seen.

The room spins, the scene changes. My little girl is a toddler. Walking through a crowd . . . when I lose hold of her hand. She disappears; I'm frantic. I turn circles, but all I see are faces. Faces I have seen before. Player number four, the hotel clerk, long blond hair and blue eyes, Rayford raising his fist. "It's not my fault!" I yell to them. "I did what I had to do to survive!"

I start awake. The nap was a mistake. The dream did nothing but deepen my depression. I head out to get some dinner. On my way, I notice a sign for a cocktail waitress. I step in and ask the waitress near the bar for an application.

"Sorry, honey," she says. "The position was filled a couple of hours ago. I shoulda taken that sign down. But you know there's an opening not too far from here at a place called Neon's."

"I don't know where that is, maybe you could give me directions."

"I'll tell you what," she said. "My shift ends in about twenty minutes. If you don't mind waiting, I'll run you over there myself."

She leaned across the bar. She had a kind face and a warm personality. She looked like she was perpetually on the verge of a hearty laugh. "You don't want to work in this dive anyway darlin'," she said to me in a confidential voice. "I sure as heck don't know why I don't get outta here. Whatcha drinkin'?"

"Nothing, thanks. I'm kind of low on funds," I added, sheepishly.

"It's on me, sweetie. Come on, make me happy."

"Well I used to love a good martini," I said.

"Naomi," she said.

"Lorelei," I said.

"Well, Lorelei, one good martini, comin' up."

She smiled at me and turned her attention to mixing my drink. I watched her work. Pretty good. She was about my age, good-looking, with dark hair and beautiful eyes. I have intuition about people, my "grift sense," I guess. I knew she was someone I would like to be friends with. I wanted to get to know her.

I felt kind of funny about taking a handout from this person. I knew I could walk out that door and in twenty minutes come back in with enough money to drink champagne all night. But I didn't want to do that anymore. At least not the stealing part. Maybe it was Father John's stories and his faith, or maybe it was the caring look on the face of my mark as I took him down. (I wonder what he's thinking about me right now?) I just wanted to try it straight for a while if I could.

We drove over to Neon's in Naomi's beat-up old Toyota Celica. My luck was no better there, job-wise anyway, but then Naomi took me out to dinner at a little dive blues bar on the north side. The décor was hideous but the ribs were great and the music was incredible. The name of the band was "Big Twist and the Mellow Fellows." I tripped over the lead singer on my way to our table. It was dark in the room and he was taking a nap under the table before they started their first set. That's what he said, anyway, when I woke him up. Could be he'd been there since their last set the night before.

"Big Twist is no longer alive," said Naomi. "He died of a heart attack some years back. The band found a new lead singer but kept the name, for obvious reasons."

The dinner with Naomi was a real tonic. Just what the doctor ordered to get my mind off my troubles. We had a great time talking and getting to know each other. And guess what she ordered, diary? Barbequed spare ribs and curly fries. Finally, I had a friend who understood the concept of ice cream and potato chips. She was a very interesting person. A friend in the making. It had been a very long time since I'd had one of those. Until I met Naomi I had forgotten what I was missing.

By the end of the evening I knew that Naomi and I were friends. There's a song that goes, "make new friends, but keep the old / one is silver but the other one's gold." Naomi is about the only precious metal I have in my life right now, so I'm happy to settle for silver.

"I have a sense about people, Lorelei Hills" said Naomi. "I know a good heart from a dark one a mile away. I am a good judge of character, always have been. It's second nature to me."

"Second nature," I echoed.

"That's right," she said. "And I judge you to be a good person, Lorelei. And you know what else?"

"What?" I asked.

"I know that you are tough. You are a survivor. No matter how far you fall, you'll always land on your feet. So take heart. Things are tough now, but I know you're gonna be okay."

I gave her a hug before I got out of the car in front of my hotel. I was hoping to see her again soon. Though something was telling me that I would not. Not right away, anyway. I flopped down on top of the bed and was asleep before my head hit the pillow.

∽

I dream. Jack of Spades, Queen of Diamonds, King of Clubs, Jack of Hearts. Jack of Spades, Queen of Diamonds, King of Clubs, Jack of Hearts. Jack of Spades, Queen of Diamonds, King of Clubs, Jack of Hearts. A child's cry. The cards are falling all around me. The vertical scar on my belly begins to burn. Searing my flesh. Insistent for my attention. The child is running down a dark alley. She is running so fast that I can't keep up with her. I am crying. Don't wake up, I warn myself. Rewind the dream and change the ending.

I am awake and I know I won't sleep anymore tonight. I have to take a walk and clear my mind. I step out onto the street. It is completely deserted and I feel a sense of serenity in the quiet. I'm calming down a little after that horrible dream. I noticed an all-night diner a couple of blocks away. I can feel the money in my pocket. Not much left, probably enough for a good breakfast and maybe lunch. But definitely not enough for another night in the fleabag. I need to get something to eat. It helps me think.

The waitress comes to the table carrying a bored expression and a pot of coffee. I push my cup toward the edge of the table so she doesn't have to waste any energy on speaking. She puts the pot down on the table, pulls her order pad out of her pocket and the pen out of her beehive and assumes a position of slouched expectation.

"Yes, I'd like the eggs over easy, hash browns, sausage, rye toast and a large orange juice."

"You coulda just said a number two."

"I know but I like saying all the food names," I say. "Oh, and could you bring an extra order of sausage? Is that link or patty, anyway?"

"Patty."

"Okay, that's fine, and, let's see . . . yeah, a stack of chocolate chip pancakes."

"Short stack?"

"No, no, a big stack. Tall stack." I can't help gesturing with my hands. I'm getting excited.

"You need an extra place setting for your tapeworm or is one fork enough?" She turns her back and shuffles as slowly as she can to the order window.

As slow as that woman walks, I am pleasantly surprised to find the food nice and hot when she finally gets it to the table. Man, this coffee's good. Okay, now where to start . . . eggs or pancakes?

❦

Well there's not much left in my pocket after that meal. But, diary, it was worth it. I feel clearheaded now. Nothing is more distracting to me than hunger. What am I going to do?

I know I can make money in a number of different ways: I could find a poker game. That wouldn't be too hard. I could make a ton of money fast and do it straight. You don't have to cheat at poker to fleece the average player. The problem is, I need a sizable stake first. I know it's not exactly a big problem, practically speaking; in a crowded city like Chicago, I could find enough marks to set me up for quite a while. But I don't want to sink back to that level again. I don't know if it's Father John's stories or Jackson's code that's working on me here, but I just can't bring myself to do it. I guess I just don't feel hopeless enough yet.

So I'll put a stake together the legit way. And fast. I'll have to; there's no margin for error here. If I don't find a job today, I'll be on the street or in a shelter tonight.

∽

Well, diary, it seems like I've just about run out my string here. There are plenty of places looking for people, but I don't have a permanent address or a phone and nobody seems to want to hire a homeless person. And I can't get an address and a phone without a job. Plus, my lack of experience in anything doesn't help. I mean, what am I going to write on an application? Well trained at pigeon drop, fan and pick, and marking cards? World class card-sharp? I'm not used to this.

I'm not used to not having control of a situation. But I'm not going to give in just yet. I am not that desperate. I can do this. What the heck; how bad could a homeless shelter be?

᠁

Pretty bad, it turns out. I've been here three nights and the women's homeless shelter is more depressing than I'd imagined. Nobody's jumping up and down and feeling good about their life. Nobody's telling uplifting stories like that preacher I hitched a ride with. Oh boy, Father John, why'd you have to go and make me feel bad about making money the only way I know how.

I think I'm starting to break. I've got to get out of here. I've got to get some money so I can get a decent meal and sleep through the night without hearing children crying and women sighing. Being here is starting to make me feel crazy. I've got to get out for a bit, take a walk out in the fresh air, away from the stink of cheap cleaning fluids, greasy hair and cigarette smoke.

᠁

That's when I saw him, when I went out for my walk. The perfect mark, a lonely-looking man alone on a bridge. All I had to do was walk toward him and pretend to fall. He'd help me up and I'd steal his wallet before he knew what hit him, and I don't care what Jackson or Father John or anybody else might have to say on the subject. I just couldn't stay in that shelter another night. I wanted to soak in a tub and get really clean. I wanted to sleep in a real bed. I wanted breakfast brought by room service. I started to walk toward him, glad I was wearing a short skirt and high-heeled boots. The legs would serve as a good distraction. He started to walk toward me.

Then, BAM! It's not me who falls. It's him.

He slips on an old beer bottle and falls flat on his back, knocking himself out in the process. I know, I know I should have taken his wallet while he was passed out, but I could still remember enough of Jackson's code of ethics to know that you never take from the weak. I hadn't descended that far. Not yet.

So, what did I do? I went to him, knelt down and gave him a slap across the face. I had to wake him up. Somebody else would steal his wallet if I didn't. Then, and this is the weird part, he opens his eyes and says, "Beth."

That's right, he calls me Beth and then he starts

pawing at me like he's drowning and I'm the life pre-server. At first, I thought he was crazy, drunk or delirious, and maybe he was all three for all I know. My instincts told me to run and I guess I should have.

Instead, I end up taking Edmund—that's his name—back to this lounge where he was singing. He starts going on about how much I look like his dead wife. For a little while he even thinks I am her. I dissuade him of that notion real fast. Then he starts asking me about my life and I tell him . . . well, parts of it, anyway. I don't tell him about my step-daddy, I may be wanted for murder. I don't tell him about Mexico, I may have been involved with a drug lord. And I sure don't tell him about my grifting days, I'm holding his wallet.

See, that was my mistake. You've got to make a clean, quick getaway and I didn't. I'd lifted his wallet before we entered the lounge, but then I stayed around for a cup of coffee. Big Mistake. I guess I just wanted to feel like a lady again, like I felt back in Mexico. But I didn't act the lady; at least I did that right. I was plain old Lorelei Hills, the girl I was before Jackson Benedict got hold of me. I poured on the accent real thick. Do the country girl thing and people think you're stupid. You can get away with a lot if people think you're dumb.

But I guess I didn't seem as dumb as I thought, because just as I'm starting to say to him that I'd better go now, he asks for his wallet back.

I smiled. I tried to make it into a friendly little joke—you know, "Oh, silly me, I thought I could get away with it." I hand him his wallet back, but as I do he grabs my hand and asks me to stay with him.

Well, you know, dear diary, if anyone else had done that to me, asked me to sleep with him after a cup of coffee, I'd have thrown the coffee back in his face. But I didn't. There's something about this Edmund fellow's touch. My whole body vibrated and for a moment I felt like I was going to pass out.

Well, I ran back here to the shelter as fast as I could. That touch—it felt really right and really wrong at the same time. I can't stop thinking about him. He's good-looking, sure, but it's more than that. Oh, stop it, stop it, STOP IT! Stop thinking about how it felt when he touched your hand. Stop writing about him. He's trouble, anyone can see that. He's got that smooth English accent and perfect manners, but if you look into his eyes, you can see he's a wolf. I've seen other men like him. You can't trust his type as far as you can throw them. Wolves prey on the weak. Forget second nature; it's their first nature. Got to stay away from that one.

I won't go back to that lounge. I'm not going to go see him again. I've got a busy day, anyhow. I've got to look for a job. I've got to get out of that shelter. I'm trying to be good, God. Can you see that I'm trying to be good? True, I kind of fell off the wagon last night, but I figure it doesn't really count because I didn't walk away with Eddie's wallet. I did walk away with a little cash, though. I guess old Eddie felt sorry for me. He threw me a few bucks, which is the reason I'm sitting in this restaurant having a ham and egg omelet right now. All they give you at the shelter is a roll and a cup of coffee. I've got a big appetite, and that's not enough for me. I've been dying of hunger practically every day since I left Mexico. I feel like a stray cat, always wondering where my next meal is coming from and how I can get more than the cat standing next to me.

Lord, this omelet tastes good. I wish I could order an extra side of bacon but I've got to buy some more clothes. This skirt and top won't be very practical when the weather starts getting cold. I'd better get some warm sweaters and long pants. Long johns if I can afford them.

I love sitting in this restaurant. It makes me feel like

a normal person. Everyone here has a home, friends and family, and they all think I do too. But the waitress is giving me the stare. Time to go, I've overstayed my welcome.

∾

I filled out seven job applications this morning. Now I'm on my way to number eight. All for restaurant work. None of them had an opening advertised in the paper but Naomi said that most restaurants don't advertise for waitresses. Anyway, I applied to all the restaurants that were listed in the paper days ago. This no-experience thing is really getting in my way. I mean, why are they going to hire me when they can hire someone who's been waiting tables for ten years? I wish I could list Nightshade, but the last thing I need is anyone knowing I was connected to Jackson Benedict.

I wonder where Jackson is right now—or if he is. I suddenly miss him so much. He was my first love. He taught me how to make love, how to make money and how to make life fun. I wish I could go back in time and live that part of my life over. Of course, I'd change the ending. In my version, nothing would happen to Jackson, nothing would happen to Maggie. We'd all go on living happily.

You left something out, blond Yoda. You told me not to die in my dreams, but you forgot to mention other people. You can't let them die, either. Tall order, but you've got to do it. If you don't, you end up alone like me.

I miss you, Jackson.

I miss you, Roberto.

∾

I look up and here I am, standing in front of the lounge where Eddie sings and plays piano. Did I know I'd be walking right by it when I turned down this street? I feel shaky, like a junkie waiting for her next fix. Will I go in or will I keep walking? I want to keep walking but I can't. My feet won't move. My mouth is dry. I feel like I'm losing my battle. I'm lonely, so damn lonely. What could it hurt, just to stop in for a minute? He and I will talk a bit, I won't feel so lonely, and I'll walk away. I can do that.

I am standing in the lobby when I hear his voice. I

like his voice. It's strong, elegant. He's arguing with someone, but I can only hear his end of it. I think he must be on the phone. I wait. I shouldn't be doing what I'm doing, and I know it. Turn around and walk away. He's no good for you. . . .

He stops talking, starts to sing. I know I am lost.

꙰

When I walked through the doorway he was singing. It was a sad love song. I watched him. He was even better looking than I remembered. He had a strong jaw, high, rounded cheekbones and sandy hair with bits of gray in it. His shoulders were broad. His music rolled over me. I stood there, breathing in him and his music. And then he looked up at me, and the spell was broken.

Boy, that was a close one. The last thing I need to do is fall for another stranger. Fall for anyone, period. I mean, love hasn't exactly worked out for me. So at that moment, I didn't really care if I stayed or if I left.

But then he starts talking about me showing up just to torture him. I don't like his tone, I don't like his attitude. I let him know that I just happened to be in the neighborhood. I was on my way to a job interview. Just wanted to see if he had recovered from his bump on the head. We go back and forth and he tells me to leave. I can't stand it when people give me orders. I guess it's from all those years with Rayford. So I decided right then and there that if he wanted me to go, I was going to stay. In fact, I was going to make damn sure that by the time I left that lounge he was begging me to stay.

That's how I got myself into trouble.

See, I knew how to get to him. Start asking him about his dead wife, this woman I'm supposed to look like. Act like I want to talk about her, for my sake. I knew he wouldn't be able to resist. It was obvious from our conversation last night that he was still at that stage in the mourning process where he was desperate to fill the void. And not only did I look like this late wife of his, I was willing to talk about her, and to let him talk about her.

Nobody dismisses me and tells me to leave. So let this be a lesson to you, Lorelei: When ego enters the picture, temptation can't be far behind.

Okay, so here's the deal. He starts talking, and I find out that he's some kind of defrocked prince. Not priest. Prince. And this Beth was his princess. He even shows me a newspaper with his picture on the front page, complete with a headline and full story about Prince Edmund. He and Beth had lived on their island paradise as benevolent rulers until his wicked half brother, Richard, deposed him. Now Eddie has no money—they confiscated his assets—and no wife. Oh yeah, and this Richard turned Beth against Eddie.

The good news is that Beth was going to go back to Edmund, because she finally realized that she still loved him desperately. The bad news is that she died in a flood before they actually got back together.

Now, of course, as I'm listening to this I'm thinking that this whole thing must be leading up to some new con game, and I'm waiting for the punchline. I may not be in the business anymore, but I still appreciate a good scam. So, here I was playing the perfect victim, and I'll admit I was getting into the story. I'm a sucker for romance, true. But the simple fact of the matter is, I had nothing to lose. I'm thinking, "If this guy is expecting to get money out of me, he's crazy. The only money I've got is what he gave me last night."

But then he asks me to pretend to be his dead wife.

This must be the payoff of the scam, I'm thinking, only I don't understand how it works. Call it professional curiosity, but I've got to hear the details now.

He wants me to pretend to be Beth so he can get his hands on her money. Apparently she was worth quite a bit on her own, but her family won't let Eddie near the estate.

Well, I didn't know if he was joking or if he was serious. But if he was serious, I knew this: I was starting to feel hooked.

That's when I knew I had to get out of there.

∾

So here I am, sitting on a park bench, trying to figure this out. On the one hand, he doesn't know I'm an ex-grifter, so why would he ask me to do this? On the other hand, if this is all a set-up, he would have had to have been working me since last night, when he called me Beth.

Is he playing me, or does he want me to play them, or both?

Let me work this out. He's either crazy or he's a grifter. If he's crazy, I shouldn't go back there. If he's a grifter, he's not my type of grifter. He preys on the weak.

Besides, I'm nervous because I still don't really understand the scam.

But then I'm also nervous because I want to do it.

I want to play his dead wife. What's that Rayford used to say? "Like giving whiskey to the Indians." Good ol' Ray—not the most politically correct guy in the world.

The bottom line is, I want to feel like I belong someplace. I want to do something I'm good at. I want to get out of that shelter. I want enough food to eat. I want to have a home by winter.

I want to walk around and think about this.

∽

I'm sorry, Father John, I can't play it straight anymore. God's not looking out for me—at least your God isn't. My God must be some Grifter God. Why else would He put someone like Edmund in my path?

∽

As I write this, I'm lying in a real, live bed. It feels so good it almost hurts. I had no idea how tired, hungry and dirty I felt until today. All I want to do is sleep, eat and sit in the tub. I'm going to stretch this out as long as I can. Edmund thinks he has to teach me to walk like a lady and to speak without an accent. What he doesn't know is I learned how to do that years ago, from Jackson. But if that's what Edmund thinks, I'm happy to oblige. I'll do the whole "Dr. Dolittle" thing. No, wait, Dr. Dolittle spoke with animals. It was the other Doolittle, Eliza, who spoke with an accent.

Anyway, a lot has happened since this morning. I went back to the lounge and took Edmund up on his offer. That's how I came to be where I am now, in Springfield, the place that Beth is from. Edmund insists that I have to soak up the surroundings. I know I've sunk about as low as I can go, but right now, I don't care. I'm not in a shelter, lying on a cot with a bunch of people screaming, and worrying if somebody is going to steal my stuff. I'm in a beautiful room in the Springfield Inn. It's one of those colonial-looking places. Queen Anne furniture, wood floors, fireplace. If I weren't here with Edmund, it would feel pretty romantic, but I've made it clear to him, this is all business. I'm not falling for him or any guy ever again. I'm bad luck for men. My history tells me that much. Plus, I don't trust Eddie—which is what I like to call him, instead of Edmund, just because it bothers him. I'll give him that much—he's fun to tease.

So here's the story. I went back to the lounge and told Edmund we had a deal. Then we started to negotiate. I pretended I wanted things that I didn't give a hoot about. I said I wanted to go back to Albemarle and wear my crown. Or rather, Princess Beth's crown. I went on and on about how I could just see all those hometown folks bowing to me. We went back and forth about that and about money and, of course, about the biggie: sex. Not that I think he expected to get sex; he's a gentleman. But he's also a man, so I thought it couldn't hurt to be absolutely upfront about the subject.

The deal we arrived at is this: I get a third of everything we bring in.

In the meantime, he's got to teach me how to look and act like Beth.

Got to go diary, Eddie's back with the hair dye.

❦

I look at the woman in the mirror, and a chill runs up my spine. I'm breathing so fast, taking such shallow breaths that I feel dizzy. I'm a blonde now. I don't like it. It's not that I'm not pretty as a blonde, I am. In fact, it somehow looks more natural than the auburn hair. But—and I can't explain what I am feeling—when I look at myself in the mirror, it's like I'm naked. I want to leave, run away.

Eddie is yelling through the door, "Who is Lizzie? When is Beth's birthdate? Who is Alan?"

I can't answer. I can't speak. I can't even think. I'm Alice, falling down a rabbit hole. I'm breathing faster and faster. I've got to stop looking at myself. I close my eyes and pretend I still have auburn hair. My breathing slows. I force myself to remember how tough I am. Big girls don't cry. They also don't let people see their weakness. I'll just keep a thick shell around me from now on. I'm not going to feel anything for any of these people, and that includes Beth.

Maybe it's the mirror. Maybe I should just stay away from mirrors for a while.

I turn toward the door and open my eyes. I answer, "Beth's daughter. February 14. Her ex-father-in-law."

There's not a hint of a shake to my voice. I sound loud and strong and easygoing. You don't have to feel bold to act bold. In fact, often times it's the other way around. You got to act something first and then you'll feel it later.

&

I don't know what that little thing was earlier. Yes, I do. I'm feeling guilty as hell. What happened to my code of ethics? What happened to my resolution to go straight? Talk about falling off the wagon. Two days ago I was turning my life around. Now look at me, I'm learning how to be a dead woman so I can con her dear family. If this isn't preying on the weak, I don't know what is.

Just stop it, okay? Stop worrying about it. This is never going to work. Nobody's going to believe I'm this Beth, no matter how good I am. And yeah, Eddie's crazy. But that doesn't mean I can't enjoy the ride.

The good news is, I've got a queen-size bed. The bad news is, I've got to share it with Edmund. This is not a good situation. I know I'm vulnerable. He's a good-looking guy, after all. I look at his form sleeping next to me and I think, "God, I'd like to have sex."

I don't want to fall in love or anything—not that there's much chance of that. Eddie doesn't exactly treat me like a princess. He's disgusted by the way I eat, walk and talk. He really only likes me when I'm not moving or speaking because then he can pretend his precious Beth is still alive. You see, as soon as I open my mouth, I break the spell. I think he hates me at moments. I think he resents that I look so much like Beth but don't act like her.

And that's the way I want to keep it as long as possible. I want to smear it in his face. I want to say it with every gesture and each countrified sound out of my mouth: "I am not Beth." I don't want a guy to fall for me just because I look like his dead wife.

And I especially don't want anyone to forget who I really am. I'm Lorelei Hills, and no one can take that away from me. I lost myself once already, and I'm not going to let that happen again.

〰

"Who is the person in this picture?"

Edmund's got these photographs pinned up to an easel in our hotel room, all the important people in his precious princess's life. He's drilling me over and over, and I've gotten good, but suddenly I can't tell him. I had them all; I knew every name. Now I can't remember any of them. Maybe something is wrong with my brain again. Maybe I'm getting that short-term memory loss thing. In fact, there are times when everything seems to be fading, when I can hardly remember my own name, let alone the name of someone I've never met before.

I wish Edmund would leave me alone for a little while.

I just finished rereading my diary again. I needed to remember everything in it. I needed to remind myself who I am. I can't lose my past again. Thank God I wrote everything down. Now I'll always have my history. Once something is written down it's binding and legal. It's forever.

Edmund is driving me crazy with these pictures. Who's this? Who's that? First thing this morning he starts in. I'm trying eat my breakfast and he's pointing at pictures with a baton. Couldn't he let me eat in peace? He's upset that I can't remember the names in these pictures. Well, I'm upset that I can't remember anything at all. I have to reread my diary every five minutes or I start getting confused.

What's worse, I get the feeling that he wants to make me into his own personal Barbie doll. That's why he wants me to start talking like Beth and remembering like Beth. He wants a Beth doll. Well, I'm not going to give it to him.

You know, that's probably it. That's probably why I can't get those names right. I don't want to get them right. I feel guilty about doing this anyhow and then I've got Eddie trying to make me into a Stepford wife.

I've had it with him—I really have. I told him I needed some memory tools, notebooks and such. As soon as he left, I cleared out of there. I'm not going back. Those pictures are the root of my problem. Especially the one of the ex-husband. I'd tell you his name but I can't remember it.

Bye-bye, Springfield.

⁓

Surprise—I'm back. Edmund tracked me down at a restaurant called Company. They've got good chili fries and good burgers. I shouldn't have eaten there, though. That was a stupid move. I should have left town first and eaten later.

But maybe things will be better now. Eddie and I had it out. I told him that I think he wants a Beth doll. He looked a little sheepish, so I know it's true. I don't know what to do. On the one hand, I want to stay, and on the other, I want to go.

Eddie keeps drilling me on the details of Beth's life.
I'm getting it all now. Mother: Lillian. Children: Lizzie,
age 11, and James, age 2. Ex-father-in-law: Alan. I
know all her friends, the places she lived, where she
went to school, her husbands (all except that one I
can't seem to remember). I even know everything her
nasty step-daddy did to her.

Bradley was his name. He died just before Beth.
Their deaths weren't related or anything. Bradley died
of natural causes; Beth died in a flood. But this Bradley
sounds like he was a real piece of work. He abused
her just like Rayford abused me. Only difference is I
stopped that bastard from raping me. Beth wasn't so
lucky. I guess she didn't have a bat handy.

∞

I spent two hours in the tub reading my diary again
and again. That's the only place I can be alone when
Edmund's here. All this stuff I'm learning about Beth
confuses me at times. Sometimes her life seems more

real than my own. It seems like every time I put information in about Beth, I lose information about Lorelei. I wonder if actresses go through this sort of thing. I've decided I'm definitely not going to tell Edmund about my little memory problem. He would just think I was nuts.

⁓

I'm all confused about her life again. The problem is that ex-husband, the good-looking blond love-of-her-life one. He's the one causing all the problems. Every time I see his picture I feel like I want to cry. He's the one who makes me feel fuzzy. I look at the rest and I'm fine; then I look at his picture, and my mind goes blank.

And I mean blank. I feel like I'm having a seizure. It reminds me of that movie, *The Manchurian Candidate*. They hypnotized this guy while he was a prisoner of war so they could control him and make him into an operative. They had him spy on our government, kill people, that sort of thing. Any time they wanted to control the guy, they'd just call him on the phone, whisper some word in his ear, and he'd drop everything to do their bidding. He couldn't control himself, didn't even know he was doing it. That's how I feel when I see this what's-his-name's picture. Just a minute, I wrote it down on a card for myself. Phillip, that's his name. Every time I see Phillip's picture, I get hazy.

❧

Stupid, stupid, stupid. I've got to be careful. I just had a kiss with Eddie. He's a really good kisser, too. As if I needed to have that information in my brain. But it's true. His lips are soft. It felt like he was drinking me in.

Stop it, let's not dwell on it. Letting him kiss me was only a ploy. He was going to throw me out because I couldn't remember anything. Well, the truth is I could remember everything, all the people, places and things in Beth's life, except that ex-husband . . . just a sec, I have to check the card . . . Phillip. I can't seem to re-member that one's name, but I didn't want to admit that to Edmund, so I played stupid to everything. Eddie snapped and started packing my bags, so I had no choice.

I came on to him. I put my arms up around his neck, pressed my body against his and begged him to help me be like Beth. Sure enough, he kisses me. I knew he wouldn't be able to resist. I look too much like the love of his life. He's still so much in love with her it's painful. I feel sorry for him, I really do. But not sorry enough that I'm going to lose my head.

∾

I keep thinking about Beth and . . . Phillip. They got together when they were teenagers, lost one another, found one another again, and then lost one another all over again. Beth may have been married to Edmund when she died, but I'd be willing to bet she still loved Phillip. I like to think that Phillip still loved her, too. Star-crossed lovers.

Another flash.

I'm sitting on a park bench, entwined with a boy of seventeen or eighteen. My head is tucked into his neck and I'm crying. His smell, his arms around me, his gentle voice, everything about him comforts me. I un-coil myself from his embrace, push my blond hair from my eyes and lift my head to look at him.

He fades, I fade.

I start breathing hard, something about that memory frightens me. Who was this boy? Why was I crying? I have no events in my life leading to this memory or leading away from it. Is there more pain in my past that I cannot recall? I have no answers for these questions. I'm not sure I want answers.

I went on the computer and there was a website that showed a video of Beth and Eddie's wedding. I've been watching it and I've finally got her voice down. I'm going to surprise Eddie. I've got to do something to wow him, because that little kiss will buy me only so much time and I still can't remember . . . Phillip's name. It's either get my Beth down real fast or sleep with Edmund—and the latter is not an option.

Eddie's thrilled by me. I did my little Beth Raines Spaulding Lemay Winslow act and he nearly fell over. Actually, the truth is he nearly cried. Sometimes I think I should just pack up my stuff and leave. I'm hurting him as much as I'll be hurting Beth's family. Oh yeah, sure, he brought it on himself, it was his idea; but still, I can't help but feel for the guy. He may be a wolf—I haven't changed my mind about that—but he's a wounded wolf. And even a wolf doesn't deserve to suffer.

∾

We had to leave the Springfield Inn because Phillip came by and that scared Edmund. He's afraid that Phillip will see me before the unveiling and all will be lost. I don't see what the big deal is, since Phillip's never going to buy my act anyway. I mean, the man was married to Beth, he had children with Beth, they were high school sweethearts. He is never going to buy this.

So why am I going along with it? I don't know. Maybe it's because I like having a partner and I like having a con to work. It reminds me of my days with Jackson. I guess that's what this is really about.

How much I miss Jackson. And how much I miss belonging somewhere.

᠁

Eddie is furious with me. He basically sent me to my room without supper. I can't seem to move without him getting upset. So, here I sit bored silly while he's sitting in Towers, the restaurant of this fine hotel, having drinks. I hate being alone because when I'm alone I start thinking about what I'm doing and how wrong it is. I know I have to put a stop to this for everyone's sake, including my own. Anyone can see that this situation has the potential to hurt a lot of people.

᠁

Eddie still hasn't come back. I'm feeling antsy. I keep thinking about my vision. The one where I am sitting with the teenage boy on a park bench. Something about it doesn't seem right. What is it? My head was tucked into his neck, I looked up and I pushed blond hair out of my eyes. That's it. I saw myself as a blonde. When was I a blonde? I don't remember that. A chill runs down my spine and I drain my martini.

❧

Where's Eddie? My head feels like it's spinning. I feel as if the walls of this room are closing in on me. I've got to get out of here so I can breathe. I've got to get out of this hotel and out of this town. I feel like I'm going crazy here.

Ever since Eddie brought me to Springfield my memory has been getting worse, not better. I'm afraid I'm losing my past. Screw it, this isn't worth it. I don't have to stay here suffocating. I'm going to put on one of those pretty dresses Edmund bought me for my Beth debut and I'm going to have one last night in Springfield. Maybe I'll go back to Mexico. My memory was getting better there. I should have gone back to see if Roberto was alive. But I couldn't. The truth is I didn't want to know that Roberto had died. I wanted to leave believing that he could still be out there somewhere.

I could have fallen in love with him. I wouldn't even care if he was a drug lord, because, hey, look at me: Who am I to judge?

I feel so much better, just having made the decision to go back to Mexico. That's the first good decision I've made in weeks. I'm excited. I have a place to go and I have a reason. In two or three days I'll know about Roberto. I hope he's still there. I hope he likes blondes.

In fact, forget leaving tomorrow. I'm leaving tonight. After I get dressed, I'll have a couple more drinks, I'll go downstairs and tell Edmund he's not the boss of me anymore. Then I'll pick up some easy money to finance my trip south.

❦

I choose the pink dress because it looks the best on me. I look at myself in the mirror. I like what I see. I am beautiful.

❦

I am half in the bag and full of myself as I step off the elevator. I am ready to tell Edmund it's time for me to be moving on. I don't care who sees me. I'm not Beth and I never will be Beth. Case closed.

Then I see him.

It's Beth's ex. Blond, chiseled features, perfect build, just like in the photographs. I'm falling through the rabbit hole again. There's nothing I can do about it, nothing I want to do about it. I know I am in exactly the right place at the right time. This con must be my destiny.

My adrenaline begins to pump. In that instant, I experience perfection in the universe. It's as if all the stars have come into perfect alignment. I want to say that it feels like I've been waiting my whole life for this moment, but that's not quite it. It feels more as if this moment has been waiting for me. The moment's not late; I am. And I am euphoric. I finally feel as though I belong.

But then it hits me. Tap, tap, tap. I'm leaving for Mexico; I'm going back to find Roberto. This scam breaks my code of ethics. How can something so wrong feel so right? Suddenly, I want to tell him I'm not Beth. I want to turn around and run, run so fast that the rabbit hole can't keep up with me, but I can't. It's no use, I know I have to let it play out. It's my fate. Mexico will have to wait.

I have only one chance to make this work. I must hope that his grief is so unbearable that he will let me fill his emptiness. I must hope that his mind will choose to overlook all that is wrong with me and see only what is right with me.

Only seconds have passed, but it seems like years. He's staring at me. I want him to make the first move. I can't play him if I can't see him move. I'm waiting—waiting for him to either call me Beth or say something, anything. I can't stand the waiting.

I step down the stairs and the con begins.

It feels as if I'm stepping into a warm bath. I go to Edmund first. I mustn't rock the boat. I know that everything depends on this moment. I want to be as perfect as the moment, but I'm not. I shouldn't have had those cocktails before I came down. I'm too giddy, giddy from the alcohol and giddy from the sensation that I belong. I told you, Father John, my God is the Grifter God. Why else would this be happening?

I feel his eyes on me—Beth's ex-husband's. I'm too light, I'm too giddy. I can't help it, it feels as though there are bubbles running through my veins. My head is telling me that he will never buy this con but, in my heart, I know something different.

As I said, it's fate. There is nothing either one of us

can do about it. I have the feeling that I could break into my thickest southern accent and it wouldn't matter. He'll believe it's Beth and I'll let him. I wait.

Then he says it—the one word I've been expecting. "Beth."

I open my mouth . . . hesitate . . . think through the thicket of gin and vermouth . . . and out it pops—first try, only try, perfection: "Phillip."

See, there never really was any choice.

Everything after that is a blur. Edmund tries to pull me into the elevator, Phillip stops us from leaving. He picks me up in his muscular arms. I feel myself pressed against his chest. Click. I can hear more stars snapping into place.

Phillip is beyond happy. I can tell he wants to hold Beth and never let her go. I am beyond happy, too, because I know now that I was right, that Phillip loved Beth as much as she loved him.

For some reason, that's important to me.

We talk about where I've been, what happened to me. I tell him how I was washed downstream in a flash flood in Mexico. He already knows that, he was down there trying to find me. Then I tell him what he can't possibly know, because I'm making it up as I go along—how missionaries rescued me, how they took me to their mission, how they nursed me back to health. Edmund is looking at me nervously, expecting me to make a mistake. Phillip is looking at me attentively, waiting for me to explain everything. Where Beth has been, why she didn't call, a million details. All the details. Details that Eddie never gave me.

I need to stall. I need to buy some time so I can figure out how to get my way through this. Which is when Phillip starts looking at me suspiciously.

Then I happen to hit on the answer. Use what you know.

"I couldn't remember a thing when I came to. I didn't know who I was." I say this with complete confidence. There it is; an explanation that covers everything. I'm back on track. I've put a little truth into this lie. I can talk about memory loss all day long. I know a little something about it.

I boldly go on. "In fact, I'm still having some problems with my memory. I've got a lot of gaps, things I still can't remember."

Phillip is relieved because it explains so much. He wants me to be Beth so badly he'll accept almost anything.

And I want to be Beth for him.

Another flash of memory. I am sitting with the teenage boy on the bench again. My head is close to his. I tilt my face up to gaze at him.

Edmund kicks me under the table. I'm jolted back to reality. I know what Eddie is waiting for, it was part of the original agreement.

"I want to get back together with Edmund," I say, casting the perfect adoring glance at Eddie.

Phillip opens his mouth, closes it. He can't believe what he's hearing. I look to Edmund. He seems to be holding his breath.

Hmm . . . something is amiss. I turn back to Phillip and see a hurt expression cross his face. Suddenly, I'm confused. I don't know if it's the alcohol or what. I keep talking to Phillip but my head is spinning. I feel like I'm starting to leave my body.

I need to get out of here and pull myself together. I excuse myself abruptly, saying, "I want to see my children tonight."

And I do, too. I can't wait to see my children. Phillip says he'll head back to the house and prepare them for the unbelievable news that their mother is alive.

◦◦◦

"I think Phillip is still in love with Beth," I say as we pull through the gates and up Spaulding Drive.

Edmund doesn't respond; he's jealous of Phillip.

Well, I don't care if Eddie talks to me or not. I'm on cloud nine because, as of tonight, I have a family. I have—

"Oh my Lord," I gasp. I'm looking up at the Spauldings' humble "commode."

For an instant I am back with Jackson. He'd laugh his head off if he could see me now. I shake my head and force myself back to the present. And what a gift this present is. It's a dream come true.

A butler escorts us through the mansion. I look down at the veined marble floors. I like the sound my heels make as I walk. Everything about this place says wealth. Lush draperies hang from the windows, works of art adorn every wall; even the air seems different here. I'm still tipsy from my cocktails, so I should be composing myself, but I can't. You'd think I really was seeing my family again. Well, not my family—a better family than that.

I have a broad smile on my face as I enter the study. Lillian, Alan and Phillip turn to us. Lillian, my "mother," runs toward me and grasps me in her arms. She begins to cry. I feel like I want to cry, too. I feel for her; I really do. As far as she knows, her only child has returned to her.

Lillian is beautiful inside and out. She has blond

hair styled almost exactly like my own. The resemblance is striking. Lillian looks more like me than my own mama. I find myself wishing she really were my mother and I feel terrible. After all, mama did the best she could, under the circumstances.

Alan, Phillip's father and therefore Beth's ex-father-in-law, is elegant and warm. He is the type of man who doesn't like to show his feelings. But I'm not fooled. I played the con for too many years. Alan is no man to be trifled with. Beneath that carefully constructed façade, there is a cold, calculating businessman. There is a brutality about him, but it is not physical. No, Alan is the consummate gentleman, and that's no act. But, then, Machiavelli was a real prince of a guy, too. Still, for a man so powerful and dignified to let down his guard and show his emotions is touching, and speaks volumes about Beth and how she was loved.

Phillip stands close, keeping watch over me. As apparent as it is that they all love me—or rather Beth—it's equally obvious that they can barely tolerate Edmund.

They leave to prepare Lizzie and James. I wait nervously, and I find myself touching the vertical scar on my belly. I still wonder if I have a child. I haven't remembered everything yet. In fact, I cannot account for any of the years between my last night with Jackson and my first morning with Roberto.

When Lizzie enters the room, there is one uncomfortable moment before she flies into my arms. I wonder what she's thinking, but then I'm overwhelmed by what I'm thinking. As her small arms go around my neck I feel a completeness I've never felt before. No, that's wrong. I have felt this before and it's not déjà vu. Maybe it's the memory of my mama's hugs or playing with my baby cousins, but I have most definitely felt this before. It is pure, unconditional love, and it settles right down into the core of my being, filling a void that I didn't really understand was there.

I feel Lizzie's hair against my cheek, her lovely flaxen tresses weaving through my fingers. It feels so familiar to my hand. Maybe because it is so much like my own.

And I am there. Brushing out my child's hair. I love playing with my baby's hair. It reminds me of playing with my dolls as a little girl. Except the dolls didn't sit there jabbering away and asking questions I couldn't answer. And the dolls never really loved me back. I am completely happy. She is turning to look at me. I realize that when I see her face I will have my answer. I will know my child. A baby's cry shakes me from my reverie. I look up to see Lillian carrying James into the room.

I feel the emotion pouring out of every heart in this room and I realize it's all for me. I know that I can't leave. It's not the opulent living. It's not breakfast in bed, or the wallet full of platinum cards. It's Lizzie. I can't bear to part with her. I know Phillip and Alan will let me stay in the mansion. They'll be overjoyed.

Until I ask if Edmund can stay, as well.

But I have to convince them because Edmund knows who I am. If he feels like he is being cut out of the picture he'll drop a dime on me faster than I could pick Phillip's wallet.

I have to convince them and I will, because I understand human nature. Even powerful people like these have weaknesses. The key ingredient to the perfect con, as Jackson would say, is to make the anticipation for pleasure so powerful that the mark is willing to accept some pain.

∽

I now live at the Spaulding mansion where Beth lived with Phillip and her children. The only thing I can compare this to is "Dallas." I didn't know people actually lived like this. There are maids, there's a chauf-feur, there's a cook and a butler. The rooms are huge, the furniture is fine. My bedroom, or rather, Beth's room is three times the size of our room at the inn. The bay window faces south and has an exquisite view of the grounds. The perfect place for me to stretch out for a nap after a nice, big lunch. There's a vanity table, just the kind I dreamed about having when I was a little girl. I walk over to look in the closet and I have died and gone to heaven. There are more clothes in this room than I've had my whole life. They are the most beautiful and finely tailored clothes I could imag-ine. And, best of all, I know that they all fit and I am allowed to wear them. No more hours of combing through racks at the second-hand shop, looking for deals.

This evening I lied to Beth's son, daughter, mother, ex-husband and ex-father-in-law. This should be wrong. I should feel guilty but I don't. Maybe I'll feel guilty tomorrow. Maybe I'll feel like a dry alkie after a night of cocktails. I don't care. Tonight I just want to thank the Lord for my good fortune. What a lucky stray I am. I got a family and a home all in one night.

I climb under the fine cotton sheets and, for the first time since I woke up in Roberto's bed in Mexico, I sleep dreamlessly.

When I wake up the next morning, I still don't feel guilty, and I know why. These people aren't weak. They're not good, either. Edmund told me. They're rotten, treacherous people. And they're wealthy. Perfect "marks." Willing participants in the circumstance of their own demise. They deserve what they get. Alan would understand . . . if it wasn't happening to him.

Look how they broke up Edmund and Beth. Those two were in love; there's no doubt about that. Edmund spends half his day in a kind of sad reverie. When I ask him what he's thinking, he just brushes me off. It doesn't matter, because I know what he's thinking. He's thinking about Beth. I know this because he gets the same sad look in his eyes when he's looking at me.

So there you have it. These people aren't good. Good people would never break up a love like that. Despite outward appearances, the Spauldings are a nasty, controlling bunch. They must be—they're loaded. You don't get this rich without hurting people. This will be their well-earned comeuppance. Payback time. It happens to everyone. I'm just the vessel. That's why it feels so right. I'm part of a bigger plan. Anyway, look around, they can afford to lose a little money.

Anything I take from them will seem like pocket change.

∾

Breakfast at the Spaulding Mansion. Eggs, pancakes, bacon, potatoes, fruit, cereal, muffins. I eat it all. I couldn't be happier. I look around the table. Lizzie and James are munching on pancakes, Phillip is noting something in his palm pilot. Lillian, who has stayed the night, just to be close, is beaming. Alan is alternately smiling at me and reading his paper. Edmund is looking at everyone with suspicion and contempt. He doesn't look happy. I don't care. I am the cat who ate the canary. I really stepped in it this time.

∾

Damn, damn damn. I had everything set in my mind. Why did I have to search Phillip out? Why did I have to get all the gory details about Edmund? Now the Spauldings, or at least Phillip Spaulding, doesn't look so bad after all. It's the reverse, in fact; he looks kind of like a white knight.

This is what I found out. Edmund was not exactly a prince when he was married to Beth. He didn't cheat on her, I don't think, but he did everything else. Beth wasn't going back to Edmund at all, she was trying to divorce him. That's how she came to be in Mexico. No wonder Phillip looked so stricken at Towers that first time I saw him, when I said I wanted to be with Edmund. And no wonder Edmund looked so anxious.

Plus, when I asked Phillip about Beth's inheritance from her step-father Bradley, it turns out that it isn't money. It's a silver mine in Colorado. Everything Edmund told me was a lie. Here I was thinking I was playing the con on the Spauldings, when all the while Edmund was playing me for a mark.

See? I was right. He's a wolf, a lone wolf at that. And do you know how wolves end up alone? They eat their young or their brides or their brothers or anything or anyone that gets too close. "Hey there, Little Red Riding Hood." So, the upshot of this whole thing is, I kicked Edmund out of the mansion and now I'm wondering if I should kick myself out, as well.

༄

This is wrong. Why do I still feel like I belong here? I obviously don't. I know I should tell Phillip the truth, say I'm sorry, pack my bags and leave. I've done some things in my life that I am ashamed of, but I've never done anything quite this bad. I've never broken the heart of a little child. Too many people were hurt when Beth died. Good people who didn't deserve such pain. The last thing they need is me twisting the knife.

I have to tell Phillip. That's what I'm going to do. I'll choose a moment when he and I are alone. I'll let him handle the kids and Lillian. I'll do it tomorrow night. Phillip is taking me out to dinner at the country club, just the two of us. It'll be the perfect opportunity. I'll have my bags packed and I'll be ready to roll. In fact, better plan, I'll have them packed and sitting in a locker at the bus station. Chances are he won't let me return to the mansion. I've got to be prepared. Winter is coming. Not that I'm going to stay up north long, just long enough to pick up some cash to get me to Mexico.

That's what I wanted to do in the first place. I never should have walked into Towers that evening. Messed me all up.

❦

It's all set. I packed a bag and sneaked it down to the bus station today. I used a piece of Beth's luggage and took some of her clothes. Maybe I should feel bad about that, too, but I don't. Considering what I'm giving up, I think it's okay. It's not as if Beth's going to be needing those bags and clothes anyhow. If I didn't take them, they probably would have been donated to Goodwill, where I'd wind up picking them out of a bin.

$\backsim$

I'm walking down the staircase to go to dinner. I look up and there he is. Phillip is waiting for me. He smiles and I can't help myself—I smile back. He's good to look at. He has those looks that tell you he was a star athlete in high school—football, I'd say. All the girls must have been after this one. For a minute, I think of Ben Williams. I wonder what ever became of him.

"Are you ready?" he asks.

"Yes," I say. Only I'm not talking about going to dinner, I'm talking about telling him the truth. I am ready. It's the right thing to do. My bags are packed. I've got a bus ticket in my purse.

160

He smiles. He has no idea what's coming. I feel bad for him. I know he'll be hurt. I'll tell him right after dinner, after my last supper. He places his hand on the small of my back and leads me to his car.

As we drive to the country club, I turn to look at him. I can see that he's happy. He senses my stare and, looking back, he smiles. I wish he would stop smiling. It's breaking my resolve. What is it with me and men who smile? I think of Roberto and Jackson. They got to me with their smiles, too.

I force myself to stop looking at Phillip. I turn to the passenger-side window, close my eyes and think of my diary. I must remember who I am. I am Lorelei Hills. I am not Beth Raines. I have no right to this man or to this life. I try to figure out what I will say. Whatever it is, I will tell him quickly. Get the pain over with fast, like ripping off a bandage.

I look out the window at the houses that we pass. People live and love in those houses. They have mothers, fathers, wives, husbands, sons and daughters. I wish I had that. Being a stray is a rough life. It takes its toll on the mind, body and soul.

I look back at Phillip; he looks at me, and there it is again—that smile. Damn. I don't want to tell him. There's a huge lump in my throat. I look out the window. I feel like opening the door and jumping out. I'd rather do that than tell Phillip the truth. In this case the truth seems a whole lot messier. I strain my neck upward and sigh, trying to rid myself of this ridiculous sadness. I barely know this man. Why do I feel so attached to him? Who is he to me? I just met him a few days ago.

"You all right?" he asks as he places his hand on my shoulder.

I nod my head. If I look at him, I'll start to cry.

"I'm just so happy to be back," I hear myself say.

Apparently, I've decided on a new plan. I won't tell him just yet. I'll wait a couple of days, rest up at the Spaulding mansion. I need to get a few good meals in me and then I'll tell Phillip the truth.

"It's a good plan," I tell myself.

"What's a good plan?" he asks.

I hadn't realized I was speaking out loud.

He's waiting. I can't answer, I can't even breathe.

I shrug my shoulders and he starts to laugh.

When we get to the country club, the first thing I do is go to the ladies' room, tear up my bus ticket and throw it away. The attendant is staring at me. I go into a stall to collect myself. I should feel worse, I should feel terrible about myself, but I don't. Because the fact is, I'm relieved that I don't have to go—not yet, anyway. I can live inside this dream a little longer.

When I return to Phillip's side, I am as giddy as I was the first night, but this time I haven't had a drink. I've been given a stay of execution. I know I still have to tell him, but it won't be tonight. I'll think about that tomorrow.

I've never been in a country club before. I don't know if they're all like this, but this one is grand in that old money kind of way. Rich wood paneling, high ceilings, polished floors. The maitre d' leads us through a series of rooms, each one with a fireplace. This must have been some magnate's home at one time. As we continue through the rooms, everyone turns to look at us. The women are smiling and the men are nodding with respect, even deference. They all seem to want Phillip's attention, but he is focusing only on me. He sees no one but me. Finally, we're seated in a small room that seems to be tucked away from everyone else. Phillip moves to hold my chair and I sit down.

We're smiling at each other across the table. He's talking, I'm talking, but I don't know what he's saying and I don't know what I'm saying. I don't care. I look down at the menu, but I can't concentrate. The words mean nothing to me. I order something. Phillip orders something. We're in our own private world—our little bubble.

Then the bubble bursts.

The waiter is looking at me, judging me, whispering to Phillip. I don't know what he's saying; too much blood is pounding in my ears. But I know what he's implying. His look tells me everything. He is saying I don't belong here. And, of course, he's right. I'm not a card-carrying member of the rich, happy-ending club. I'm waiting for disgust to cross Phillip's handsome features. I have been exposed. I hold my breath and think of the shredded bus ticket.

Then Phillip looks at the waiter. His expression says everything: "One more word and I'll have you fired." The rat scurries away.

Phillip turns his face to mine, thoughtful and attentive. Click. Click, click, click, click. More stars exchange places. I think back to the planetarium. Maybe the warrior can rescue the princess, after all.

Phillip and I laugh, and talk. We smile a lot. I try to be as Beth-like as I can be. I try to be as elegant as Beth, but it's no use. I'm having too much fun. I can't hold myself back. I'll never be as reserved as Beth, not while I'm feeling this happy.

Next surprise: Phillip likes it. He's laughing with me. I make him happy. I think of Ben Williams. I think of Sue Ann Kurlin. I see Edmund enter the room.

It's obvious that Edmund came here looking for me. I'm disappointed but not surprised. I knew this was coming. I didn't really think I could get away from him. I made a deal with the devil and now he expects me to hold up my end of the agreement.

I pretend not to notice Edmund. I put my focus completely on Phillip and try to forget about Edmund. But it's no good; the lone wolf won't leave. And when Phillip gets up from the table to make a call, Edmund pounces.

He starts threatening me and reminding me of our deal. Fortunately, Phillip returns before the scene gets too ugly, and Edmund has no choice but to leave. I try to get back into the fantasy. I want to believe that I'm really Beth, that her charmed life belongs to me. But it's no use, it's time to pay the piper.

I've been avoiding Edmund. Big mistake. The only smart thing I've done lately is leave that packed bag at the bus station. I'll be needing it real soon. I've got to confess to Phillip and get out of here. And not just to protect the Spauldings. Once the truth is known I'll have destroyed all of their lives. No little girl should have to mourn the loss of her mother twice. But I have to leave to protect myself, too—and I don't mean from prison. At least not the kind of prison that has bars. If I stay too many more days, I'll start getting attached.

Who am I kidding? I am already attached. To the family of my dreams.

∽

I've been reckless. I've broken every rule I was ever taught about working a con. What would Jackson say if he saw me now? His little protégé is turning out to be an embarrassment. I've agreed to let Alan, Phillip and Lillian give me a "welcome home" party. Big mistake. Not that I could exactly refuse. They're so happy to have me home, they insist on doing things for me. There's the real reason you're not supposed to prey on the good or the weak: They kill you with kindness.

∽

They asked me what kind of party I wanted. I chose a costume ball. Wearing a mask seems appropriate right now. I should be dressed as something awful, but I chose a princess. I'm not ready for them to see my true colors yet.

I watch myself in the mirror as I step into my blue satin gown. I study the sequined bodice as I reach back to close the zipper, and when I look up, I'm transformed.

I'm a princess.

At least for tonight.

The party was good and bad. I'll get to the bad part later. The good part is that everyone was wonderful to me. The party couldn't have been better. Not that I'm an expert on big glamorous parties, since this was my first. They rented out Towers, the place I first saw Phillip. Everyone was there. I have great friends—I mean, Beth has great friends.

Remember who you are: You're Lorelei Hills.

Alan is shouting, "Speech, speech."

"Speech!" they're all saying. "Speech! Speech!"

I look around. Everyone's staring at me. Phillip is looking at me with a mixture of love, pride and support. I hesitate; I don't know what to say to these loving people. I've never been a part of anything like this before. Phillip gives me a look that seems to say, "Are you all right? You don't have to do this if you don't want to."

But I smile and take the floor. My warrior prince stands beside me, ever ready to defend. The moment is perfect.

I scan the room as I bask in the heartfelt applause of so many wonderful people. The moment is perfect—until I see Edmund. That was the bad part.

∽

I'm lying in bed, looking up at the ceiling. I have to meet with Edmund this morning. I can't put him off any longer. He threatened to expose me if I don't get back to the plan. I can't go through with it and I can't just walk away either. I need to buy some time so I can figure out what to do. I cannot bring myself to break the hearts of Lillian, Phillip and my . . . no, Beth's two beautiful children.

I'm living in a fairy tale. But not the one I imagined. It's the original version. The one that was there before the Hollywood people got hold of it and gave it a happy ending. In the original, the middle is happy and the ending is sad. That's how all fairy tales used to be. Their purpose was to prepare little girls and boys for lives of disappointment. This ending is not going to turn out well, I've already seen to that. I can't untell the lies that I've told. But, there's got to be a way to soften the blow and I've got to find it.

I'm entering Jackson's nightmare scenario. I'm trying to run a con on a con—Edmund. The potential risks are high and the rewards are few. Not the ratio you look for when you're scouting a "mark." But I've made my decision. There's no turning back. There's no running away. I have to play it out to the end. I've really stepped in it this time.

 ∾

Okay, here's the plan I laid out to Edmund at breakfast this morning. I convinced him that instead of just getting Beth's money, we should try for Phillip's money, too. This means I'll have to divorce Edmund—or rather, Beth will divorce Edmund—marry Phillip, and then divorce Phillip. I get a nice tidy settlement in my divorce with Phil and I split it with Eddie.

Of course that means staying in the mansion for a little while longer while we set up the new plan. He was not happy about that but his greed got the better of him and he took the bait. He's not as good a con as he thinks he is. But none of us is. I forgot that lesson. That's how I got myself into this mess.

This is the first con I've ever run where I am supposed to end up the loser. My goal is not to marry Phillip. The payoff I'm looking for here is to prepare everyone for my inevitable departure. I want to lessen the pain I'm going to cause. The risk is that I end up getting too close to them. That I end up more attached and entwined in this family than ever. That I destroy them and myself in the process.

This is turning out to be much harder than I thought, I reflect as I gaze up at Phillip's strong profile. We are walking in the woods, talking about "our" friends. Suddenly, he turns me to him, and cups my face in his hands. He's looking into my eyes like I am the thing he wants most in the world. I want him so much I could cry. He bends his head to kiss me. I can feel his lips even before they touch mine.

But at the last moment, I pull away. The confused look on his face almost kills me. I can't let him kiss me, ever. I can't spend time with the children. I can't spend time with Lillian.

I have to get the situation under control.

I said I'd stay away from the kids. I said it would make it easier on them when I left. So why do I continue to spend so much time with them? Do I enjoy torturing myself? I've started getting up in the middle of the night so I can watch them sleep. I know I shouldn't be doing this. But I can't help myself. Every night I tell myself, "I'm not going to go in there again." But I do. I keep thinking of the day I'll have to leave them for good. I want to press them into my memory so I'll never forget. I want to remember Lizzie and James. I don't want to have to read about them in my diary to remember.

Sometimes I feel jealous of Beth. Sometimes I wish I could keep living her life forever. I know I shouldn't think this way; it only leads to madness.

Well, look at the bright side: Suddenly Eddie seems to be looking at me in a whole new way. He keeps coming up with excuses to see me and then the other day he tried to kiss me. That's not so bad. It's good to have options. He may not be Mr. Right but could be a pretty good Mr. Right Now.

∽

Oh man, I'm in way over my head. I thought I was fine. But I'm not fine, I'm falling in love. Either that or I've got a serious case of the flu. Every time I see Phillip my heart starts racing and I feel lightheaded. He's the only thing I think about. I find myself walking down hallways hoping I'll run into him. I make excuses to go talk with him in his room at night. My whole being lights up when I'm in his presence. Whenever I'm with him, I'm happy. Whenever I'm away from him, I'm miserable.

And the thing that makes it worse is I think he's falling in love with me, too. He asks me to take walks with him every night. We walk around the grounds of his estate and we just talk and talk. We lose track of time. Sometimes we take the kids and sometimes we go alone. When we go alone, he always holds my hand. I tell myself, "It's not a big deal, him taking my hand. He was married to Beth once, it's probably just force of habit." But it doesn't feel like force of habit, it feels like . . . what's that saying? Something about hand in glove? That's how perfectly our hands match. That's how natural it feels. My hand feels more natural in his than it does on its own.

∽

Lillian gave me a letter today. She said she wrote it when she first got the news from Mexico that her daughter was lost and presumably dead.

Dear Beth,

Today I received the worst news a mother could ever receive in her life: that you were really and truly gone. They said it was hopeless—that even if you'd actually survived the ravages of the flood, you would have died of exposure in the desert by now, or from starvation, or been killed by one of the wild animals that roam the desert.

But you see, my darling, I don't believe any of this. I believe that if something like that had happened to you, then I would know it. A mother and daughter have a special bond that goes deeper than almost any other bond I can imagine. It goes deeper than the bond of husband and wife, for mother and daughter share the same blood. They are bound up not only emotionally, but also in some way that transcends feelings. They are cut from the same cloth, and it is a cloth that can never rip, can never shred, no matter how much anyone pulls on it or tries to tear it to pieces.

I don't believe you're gone. You can't be gone. You and I are still one. I wait for you to come home. It is the only thing that keeps me going.
All my love forever,
Mom

I think it's safe to say I made a big mistake. How could I have ever thought this was possible? No amount of distance will ever lessen their pain when they find out that Beth is truly gone. All I have done is deepen their joy and I've allowed their wounds to heal over, knowing that I will soon rip them open again. This time they might not heal. The heart can only take so much breaking. And I've let myself fall in love with them, as well. I have exposed myself to having my heart broken. And I know it will be. But that is only the punishment I deserve.

Father John, you were right after all. I should have stayed on the straight.

∾

I'm looking into Phillip's eyes. He has just given me a present—a Tammy Wynette CD. There are tears in my eyes. I want to cry because I love him and I will be breaking his heart. He is the best man I have ever known. I feel that I should spend the rest of my life by his side. I feel that I belong to him. He holds my face in his hands. I move to him. He moves to me. We are inches apart. I pull away.

I don't want him to kiss me. He will be kissing Beth, not me. And, as much as I long to feel his lips caress mine, I know that I don't deserve it. He is too good for me. He is honest and clean. I am a con and I'd be conning myself to think I am anything different.

°

∽

Lizzie and I are playing dress-up, just like I did with mama when I was a little girl—one of the few good memories I have from my childhood.

"You're different, mommy," she says. "You're fun. You don't seem so sad anymore." Little does she know the private torture I feel. But in that moment all my pain disappears and I want to scoop her up and squeeze her. She has said the one thing I needed to hear. She loves me for the things that make me different from Beth.

I hold a special place in her heart. Me, Lorelei. At that moment, I know I will never leave. I must fight to stay. Who cares that I seem to lose a little more of Lorelei every day? Lose a past, gain a future.

Phillip enters the room. He teases us about the makeup and chases Lizzie out. He returns and I am on cloud nine. He is looking at me with love and I am returning it. He likes me just the way I am, too. We are in our own private world. I break the spell. Without even realizing it I have said something about Edmund that Beth could not know. Incredible, I can't remember I'm Lorelei and not Beth half the time, but I can remember some stupid song Edmund sang in Chicago.

Lizzie saves me. She asks me to put her to bed.

When I return to the room, I'm sure Phillip will look at me with suspicion, question me. He does not. He wants to stay in the middle of the fairy tale as much as I do. He's not ready for a sad ending either.

I want him to kiss me. I am ready for it now. He is sitting next to me looking down. I can see that he will not try to kiss me again, even though he wants to. I have pushed him away twice already. He is trying to control himself. I lean in, close enough to let him know I am ready for his kiss, close enough to smell his scent. The scent is somehow familiar. A reminder from my past? I brush this thought away. I am interested only in the present. I lean in closer and whisper his name. We are almost touching. He cannot control himself; I cannot control myself. We have waited too long. He turns to me, our lips come together and all the stars click into place.

❦

I am sitting at the breakfast table. Everyone is here—
Alan, Lizzie, James, Phillip, even Lillian. Everyone is
talking except Phillip and me. We are just looking at
one another and smiling. We have a secret that no one
else shares. We are in love.

∽

Everything is falling apart. Phillip is getting increas-
ingly impatient for my memory to return. I'm making
too many slips, important things that I should have
known, like Lillian's breast cancer. Soon Phillip will
realize that there is no more memory coming back . . .
that I am not Beth. I don't want it to end yet. I don't
want it to ever end.

∽

Phillip wants to take me back to Mexico so that I can
get my memory back. He wants to find the mission
where I recovered. Of course, there is no mission.
There is nothing for me in Mexico but loss. I lost Roberto there just a few short months ago and now I will
lose Phillip there as well.

Phillip thinks he's helping us push our relationship along. And he is. He's bringing it to an end. He wants me to be whole so we can marry. He wants to help me get well. I want to scream, "Don't you know what you're doing? You think you are making me whole but you're tearing us apart." I want to stop this from happening.

୦୦

I have to get myself together. I can't let fear take over the situation. There's a way out of this and I know I can find it. After all, my entire life, what I can recall of it, has been about beating the odds; about turning liabilities into assets. Life and history are full of stories about triumph in the face of defeat. And like the saying goes, winners never quit and quitters never win. The people who get what they want in this world boldly reach out for the brass ring, willing to risk falling off the horse.

Phillip Spaulding is the perfect example of this idea. He has never shied away from a battle or a challenge in his life. And neither have I. That's why I know that we are meant to be together. That's why I know that I have to fight to stay in his life. I just can't pass up a chance at the brass ring. I may not ever get another.

∽

I never stop being amazed at the opulence of the Spaulding lifestyle. I was nineteen years old before I ever flew in a plane. That was the year Maggie and I went to Florida on vacation. Now, I'm sitting in a limousine driving onto the tarmac of an airport. I'm about to board the Spaulding Enterprises jet. I wonder, diary, if you could speak, would you fault me for wanting to stay? Is the lie so bad when the result of success would be a happy ending for everyone?

Phillip takes my hand and leads me across the runway to the jet. I enter the plane and settle into my seat. I am feeling a little tired. I sit back, close my eyes and try to relax as the jet takes off and turns toward Mexico.

∽

I am intoxicated with wine and desire. Drops of sweat bead up in the valley of my breasts. It is too warm for clothes in Mexico tonight. I unzip my dress and let it fall to the floor. Even my black silk slip clings to my body. His eyes are on me, as I tilt my head back toward the ceiling fan and let the breeze from the slowly turning blades cool my glistening skin. I lift the hair from the back of my neck, close my eyes and sway to the sensual thrumming of a Spanish guitar coming from the plaza below. Lost in the music, I let myself breathe in the musky perfume of the exotic night. His desire is palpable, rising in unison with my own. My eyes open and I beckon him toward me. He crosses the room and takes me in his arms. . . . My hands slide over his tanned, muscular chest. He pulls me to him and we move as one. The heat of his body excites my unrequited desire. In our urgent longing, we tear the remaining clothes from our bodies. Cupping my face with his hands, he brings his lips to mine. I guide him to me as I lay back onto the bed. I feel his naked body moving against mine, our long, denied hunger is released and we are one. He whispers my name, "Beth."

I wake with a start. It was only a dream. Embarrassed by my fantasy, I look at Phillip. He is completely unaware of my thoughts, but somehow I still feel shame. How could I have imagined him so vividly. We've never made love, yet I know exactly how it feels to be with him. My body is still tingling with excitement from his "touch." This felt more like a memory than a dream. I cannot contain myself.

"Phillip, have we ever made love?" I blurt out.

He looks at me with amusement and concern. "Of course."

I stare at him, not believing until it dawns on me— he is talking to Beth, not Lorelei. I cover by pretending I've just made a very funny joke, but inside I am hurt.

∽

Phillip keeps asking me questions. Do I remember this? Do I remember that? Well, of course I don't, but he is convinced that being in Mexico will jog my memory. Why do these memories have to be so damn important to him?

He has insisted that we stay at the same hotel Beth stayed at before she died, even though there is only one room available. I wonder who gets the bed? Tomorrow he will begin searching the missions for anyone who might know Beth. I have already told him that I don't want to go. I'm hoping that I can keep him from going as well.

∽

It's strange, diary, I keep thinking that I saw Roberto today. While I was walking in the plaza, I saw a man who looked like him. But he was far away and I could not see his full face. I wanted to call out his name but Phillip was with me and I would have some explaining to do. I'm probably being ridiculous. Mexico is a big country and I'm a long way from San Miguel.

∾

I'm lying in bed, Phillip is beside me, and this time it's not a dream. We're not lovers, although I want to be. We are just sharing a bed because there's no other place to sleep. I thought we could be adults; there's no sense in him sleeping in a chair. But now I wonder. I keep thinking of that dream. I desperately want to make love to him. My body is tense with desire. I feel my heart race with the thought of his skin against mine.

I look to Phillip. He is on his side; his back is to me. I know he is not asleep, I know he is having the same problem sleeping as I am. I want to reach out and touch him.

"Phillip," I say softly, "Are you asleep?"

There is a pause. "No," he answers.

I can feel his desire, it radiates out from his body like heat from the sun. But he is trying to pull himself back. He wants to wait until my memory fully returns. It will never return and I cannot wait.

I reach out and touch his shoulder. I hear an intake of breath. I run my fingertips down his arm.

"Phillip," I say again. He shakes his head slightly and exhales. He knows what I am asking. I pull myself closer to him, so that my body lightly grazes his.

"Why do we have to wait? Why do we have to torture ourselves? Why do I have to wait to relive what I have lived so many times before?"

"Beth, it wouldn't be right."

"Why?" I say as I lean down and kiss his neck. I am not giving up that easily. I'm Lorelei Hills, I go after what I want. God helps those who help themselves, right? I want this man to finally give in to me. I have the feeling that if we make love, all the things he thinks I can't remember won't matter.

"I want you to make love to me," I say as I continue to caress his arm and kiss his neck. I can feel his resolve is breaking.

"Just kiss me once," I whisper.

My lips are near his cheek. I wait. He turns to me slightly and I have my chance: I lean down to kiss him. We are hungry for each other. We have waited for so long. His hands hold my head as we kiss. I press my body to his and our hands begin to explore one another. Then he pushes me away.

"I can't do this," he says softly as he gets up and walks away.

I close my eyes and sigh. I can see by the firm set of his profile that there is no use protesting. He believes with all his heart that my memory must return before we can move ahead. He is such a good man. His denial is all about protecting me, or rather, Beth. How can you not love a man like that?

I am sitting in the bathroom of our hotel room writing this down. Phillip has left and he will not be back tonight. He insists on finding the damn mission where Beth recovered. He's like a dog with a bone on that one. I did everything in the book to get him to stay here and spend the day with me. Nothing doing. He just kept saying that this is something that he needs to do. He says that I must get my memory back.

"Why?" I said. "Maybe it's for the best. Sometimes people forget painful memories in order to survive. The mind and the heart can only take so much." And what I said is true, too. You hear about people all the time who go off wandering for days after witnessing a traumatic event. It's our mind's way of protecting us. But Phillip does not share my belief. He insists that he has to do this. He feels it's the only way I, I mean Beth, can be whole again.

After he left, Eddie showed up, which is the reason I'm sitting in the bathroom. We had a fight. He says he took a flight down here to protect the plan. But, I wonder if it's the plan or me that he is worried about. He keeps telling me that Phillip is no good for me. He says that Phillip is only interested in Beth, not me, not Lorelei.

Does he realize how much it hurts me when he says things like that? How could he know what is in Phillip's heart? He was not there last night to see the longing in Phillip's face, to feel his body respond to even my lightest touch. It wasn't Beth Phillip was kissing, it was me. It wasn't Beth he desired, it was me. He has fallen in love with me, not Beth. Sure, Beth was the mother of his children. Phillip and Beth had a long history together. But they weren't married anymore. He didn't love her, but he's in love with me, my version of Beth.

I can hear Eddie yelling to me outside the door.

"Lorelei, please come out and talk to me. I'm sorry I upset you. You have got to believe that. I want what is best for you. For us. Phillip's not like us. He loves you because he thinks you're someone else. I love you because you can act like you're someone else. He always does what's right. We do what we have to do, whether it's right or not. He has no secrets, we have nothing but secrets. You could never be happy with him in the long run because you're not like him. You're like me. Don't you want someone who can appreciate you for what you are?

"Lorelei, please come out and talk to me."

You know, diary, Eddie's right. I am more like him than I am like Phillip and there's no use denying it. It's probably wishful thinking to believe that I could ever completely fit into Phillip's world. And the truth is, Eddie's not such a bad option. We are alike, as I said, and I can always depend on him. I mean, look at this situation. I'm in a bind, Phillip's about to find out and Eddie jumps on a plane and flies down to Mexico to help me out. Yeah, yeah, yeah—he's after the Spaulding millions, but, it's more than that and we both know it. Eddie has become my friend. I realize that now. Who else in Springfield could know my secrets and still care about me? Certainly not Phillip or any of the Spauldings.

"I'm sorry about before," I say sheepishly as I come out of the bathroom. Eddie is still there. He has been waiting for me.

"It's okay." He responds nodding his head. "I understand."

And in that moment, I see that it's true, he does understand. He knows that I have fallen for Phillip. He could tease me about it, he could make me feel like a fool—but he doesn't. Instead, he takes my hand and leads me to sit next to him on the bed.

"I know how difficult this has been for you. I know that you're a sensitive person even though you try not to show it. I'm almost sorry I got you into this. But, you have to make a choice. I need to know, what's it going to be—continue the deception with me or end it all now?"

At that moment, I realize he knows me better than anyone. He sees through me. I am filled with emotion and I want to wrap my arms around his neck and ask him to hold me while I cry, but I don't.

"Eddie, what makes you think I'm not on your side? This hasn't been hard on me, I don't know what you are talking about. I don't care for Phillip. I'm trying to bring this con back into focus. I'm trying to rescue the situation."

He just looks at me. He knows I'm lying. I start to turn away in embarrassment. Just at that moment, I hear a clap of thunder and I jump into Edmund's arms.

"I don't like thunderstorms," I say shyly.

"It's okay," he responds as he strokes my hair. After a moment I pull back from him. Eddie is looking at me with amused surprise. . . . Then he smiles and gently takes me back into his arms. He comforts me as I lean my head against his shoulder.

I hear him sigh. I draw back to look at his face and I can see the sadness in his eyes. I can see that Eddie is hurting, too. We are both in love with people we can never have. He is in love with Beth and I am in love with Phillip. At this moment, we understand each other better than any other two people in the world.

I reach up and stroke his cheek.

"Eddie, tell me about Beth," I ask. "Tell me about your life together."

Eddie pauses and breathes another deep sigh. He smiles gratefully at me, and we lay back on the bed, my head on his chest as he begins the story of his lost love.

As I listen to him, to the sound of his voice, I realize

how comforting his presence has always been to me. And for the first time I think to myself, "maybe I *could* make a life with this man." He may not be prince charming, like Phillip, but he accepts me as I am, warts and all.

When Edmund finishes speaking I can see a lightness about him that was not there before. It is as if he has released a great weight from his shoulders. I believe that he has released Beth. He looks down into my eyes and smiles—he is free. I tilt my head up to his and our lips become one.

It is a beautiful kiss: deep, honest. There are no lies, no secrets. We pull back to look at each other. There is a new understanding between us. I tuck my head back into his chest and fall into a dreamless sleep.

∾

I woke up this morning, alone. Edmund left in the night and Phillip has still not returned. I think he is avoiding sleeping in this bed with me. I miss him.

As I lie here thinking about my life, I realize that everything I am I have learned through my relationships. Roberto, Ben, Jackson, Edmund and Phillip have all played a part in bringing me to this moment. They all taught me something important. But I have only now put it together.

Roberto showed me that there is a difference between being vulnerable and being weak. When we are vulnerable, we open ourselves to lives of fulfillment. Only through remaining open can we experience love, sensuality and joy. Weakness is what causes us to run away from these things.

Ben taught me that life can be unfair and that people can be cruel. Even so, it's not what happens to us that matters, it is what we do with it.

Jackson taught me how to be whoever I need to be in the moment. We all have many different faces, how we use them determines the experience of our lives.

Edmund taught me that what we dislike in others is just a reflection of what is unpleasant in ourselves. I resisted acknowledging his love—not because he is wrong for me, not because he is all bad, but because we are weak in some of the same ways.

Phillip taught me that nothing is more important than the relationships in our lives. They are what make life worth living.

But I have contorted these lessons. I know why I was involved with these men, but I lacked the courage to change. That is why I find myself here in Roberto's sensuous country, feeling ashamed, working the grift with another lost soul while I wait for love.

With this newfound clarity, I feel that I am on the verge of more memories. I am excited by the thought of where this knowledge may take me, but I am also frightened. I am torn completely in two by these opposite feelings. I feel there is a struggle ahead. I can only guess at the final outcome. Life has been a surprise to me up to this point, I am sure it will continue to be.

∽

Time has passed and I am back in Springfield. I have had no time to write, or maybe I did not want to. An experience in Mexico has left me feeling shaky.

I was, once again, lying to Phillip, trying to play a part that was not mine to play. We hired a troupe of actors, Huevos Rancheros was the name of the company, to portray the nuns and priest that had nursed Beth back to health in their mission. It was a poorly hatched plan with an untrustworthy cast but, somehow, Edmund and I were able to pull it off. I was invigorated by my deception while at the same time I

felt repulsed. I wanted to run. As this struggle was oc-
curring inside me, I heard bells chiming. Suddenly, I
was transported to another place and time. I was at a
mission, being taken care of. A nun was saying: *La esperanza es lo ultimo que se pierde.* "Hope is the last
thing you lose."

Where was I? When was I there? I do not understand this vision and it frightens me. I want to run
away from everything I learned in Mexico. Whatever
my life has been to this point, I feel safer retreating
to the old me, someone I already know and understand.

෴

What do I want? Who do I want? I suddenly find
myself deeply attracted to both Edmund and Phillip.
Edmund calls to the part of me that wants to remain
who and what I am. Phillip calls to that in me which
wants real and honest communion with others. I feel
that whichever of these men win out will seal my
fate.

I remember once before I said that the con with
Edmund is like stepping into a warm bath, and it is.

There is such a comfort to familiarity. I know that he loves me. I love him, too. My love for him is like accepting a side of myself that others may call ugly. At the same time, other parts of him call on me to grow and be stronger. I don't know what will happen between us. I wish Father John were around. I'd ask him if he could tell me what to do. Of course, the answer he'd give me probably wouldn't be the one I wanted to hear. What did that bumper sticker say? "Sometimes the answer is no."

∾

I believe Phillip is going to propose to me and I am going to say yes. I don't know if I'll be saying yes to him or to Edmund. You see, I have written Phillip a love letter, which Edmund helped me to compose. The purpose of this letter is to push Phillip's emotions to the point where he wants me to be his wife. The thing is, dear diary, I want to be Phillip's wife. I want the courage to take all I have learned and change. I know that if I marry him, I will be able to do that. But I also want to stay with Edmund. I can't let go of him. He makes me feel secure. I have the strangest fear that if

I lose Edmund, if I become completely involved with Phillip, I'll die. Isn't that stupid?

⤳

I have decided that if I must, I will let go of Edmund, and in doing so, I'll let go of a side of myself. I am ready now. I want a life with Phillip. Edmund may be more like me, but in Phillip I see everything I can become.

⤳

I've checked myself in the mirror more times than I can remember. I want to look perfect at the moment he asks me. I can barely contain my joy. Soon I will be Mrs. Phillip Spaulding. I'll have my happy ending.

⤳

I enter the study to see Phillip reading my letter. He looks up at me, filled with emotion. Eyes brimming with tears. I feel as if I could cry as well. I love this man, there was never really any doubt. I want to belong to him.

As I walk to him, he looks back down to the letter. I grasp his right hand and move my body close to his. I breathe him in; his scent intoxicates me. I wait expectantly. He reaches into his pocket. When he withdraws his hand I expect to see my diamond ring. Instead, I see a flyer, the words Huevos Rancheros boldly written across the top. He looks back up at me. There is no love in his eyes. "Who are you?" he says. For a moment, I stand confused. He waits. Then it hits me—the tears in his eyes are not for me, they are for Beth. My house of cards collapses around me. The day I have been dreading since I first met Phillip at Towers has arrived. He knows what I am and I am crushed. My carefully constructed fairy tale, the Hollywood version, is over. There will be no happy ending. Every night before I go to bed I have been telling myself not to die in my dreams. I should have been telling myself every morning as well.

～

I wake up in my bedroom, but it's not my bedroom anymore. Phillip had the decency to let me stay one more night. I cannot bring myself to leave this life. I must convince Phillip that I can be Beth—for him, for the children, for Lillian—forever.

I'll make Phillip believe that this is no longer a con. That the con ended a long time ago. I'll make him believe that I truly love him and that he loves me. I can make him believe it because I know that it is true. My heart breaks. It's only now that I realize how much I have lost.

❧

It's over. Phillip kicked me out. No more costume balls. No more games with Lizzie. No more embraces from the man I love. It is a recurring theme in my life. Every man I have ever loved has been taken away from me. Each loss, another wound to my heart. But this time there will be no scar. This time the wound will not heal.

❧

I'm writing this on a plane somewhere over America. Out the window, clouds drift below us in fragments. In here—in my mind—fragments of thought drift by, too. Beside me in seat 16D sits Eddie, asleep with his head tilted to the side and his mouth half open. I wonder what he dreams about: Does he picture me in his dreams? Does he picture the kind of life we'll have together after all of this is over?

Me, I can't picture it.

I try, I really do, but somehow the thoughts end up in little pieces, wisps of clouds floating through open space. We're here, the two of us, and we're heading to Colorado, and I suppose I should feel lucky that it's worked out the way it has. At least we're not in jail.

But I don't feel lucky. Nothing ever works out the way I expect it will; the way I hope it will. I can't recall a time in my life when happiness stayed around. A time when the world stayed fully lit up. Sue Ann Kurlin ruined my time with Ben. Gunshots ended my time with Jackson and Roberto. But in some ways this is the worst. I have only my own deceit to blame for the loss of Phillip, Lizzie, James and Lillian.

My life has been one long, endless session at a gaming table. The chips have fallen where they may, and there have been some losses, some wins, but the over-all feeling right now is numbness. That's what all gamblers feel at the end of the day. Finally, even when they've got a big stack sitting in front of them, tall as a tree, they don't really notice. They ask themselves: Who cares?

I guess I've won this game—this con. Eddie's won, too. We're about to collect exactly what we set out to win when we concocted this whole scheme back in Chicago: Beth's inheritance. We're heading to Colorado to claim the silver mine, and this should give me some kind of rush—but it doesn't, not really.

We're a team, Eddie and I, and this, too, should give me a rush. But again, it doesn't. The flight attendant, a tired blonde, just came by with the drinks cart, and I ordered a Johnnie Walker and settled back against the seat, trying to feel the heat of the alcohol as it moved down my throat.

But there was no heat. No heat, no light, no deep moment of release. Just an empty sky inside me, a sky drifting with clouds. I drain the drink and set it down on the tray table. So much has happened. Strange things. The strangest thing of all. Something I want to write about, if I can find a way. If I can ever find the nerve. But it's time to close this diary for a while and get some shuteye. Eddie will be waking up soon.

The flight's half over now. The pilot just came on the P.A. and said something in his deep piloty voice about what beautiful flying weather we're going to have for the rest of the trip. The announcement woke Eddie up. He blinked, yawned a few times, then took my hand and held it in his. We kissed a little, just a few pecks, like to show that we're both here for each other—both on the same page, so to speak. He asked me if I'd been asleep, too, but I said no and left it at that. I didn't want him to know how much I've been writing in the diary, how urgent it feels to me. Even now, he's at the back of the cabin, waiting for the men's room to be free, so I guess I have a little more time to write. There's a lot to say.

First off, I was really sick in Springfield. So sick that my head was pounding and the sweat dripped from my brow as if I was a miner back in Albemarle. My fever was so high that I was scared to stick a thermometer under my tongue for fear of what it would tell me. I knew the mercury would shoot so high that I should have gone to the hospital and get an antibiotic and an I.V., but I didn't want to do that.

So I just tolerated the feeling. I pretended it wasn't

there. Part of me has always felt the need to pretend I'm fine. *You're okay, Lorelei, everything's cool. Just keep moving.*

My fever is the reason I haven't written in this diary in a while. I don't think I could have written when I was sick if I'd tried. So much happened so fast, and the sickness swept over me all at once. I was fine one minute and the next I was cold and parched and unsteady; I tried to write my name, and it came out looking like the marks made by an EKG.

The last time I tried to write something was way back before I got sick. I was sitting at Company and my cell phone rang. It was Lizzie, and the minute I heard her voice my heart and my head felt as though they were going to crash all at once. I gripped the cell phone hard because it was something substantial to hold onto. I wanted to be her mother so much. Just the sound of her voice was enough to throw me off balance, to make me almost break down. *Dear God, I told myself, don't do that. Stay strong. Strong for Lizzie.*

So I did. I sat there and listened while she told me that something was wrong with Daddy. I insisted that no, no, he was fine. I don't know if she believed me or not. All I heard was the dead hum of the cell phone, the hum of the empty space all around us. The loneliness of the distance that separates two people—the unbearable distance.

I wanted to remind her of the good times we had together. I wanted to connect with her in this way so that, at least, she could always hold onto the memory of this conversation. She could take it away for the rest of her life, and remember that even though so much of what I'd done had been a fraud—a smoke-screen, a dumb game that she couldn't have understood because she was a kid in a grownup world—she could at least think back on the times we had together and know that the feelings I had were real.

Because they were, Lizzie. I swear to you, they were. You'll never read these pages, but I tell you with my whole heart that I loved you. And that I love you still.

She didn't understand what I was saying to her on the phone, or *why* I was even saying it. How could she? She's so young. Her voice is fragile, and some-times it's like it's going to break in half in the middle of a word, and whenever that happens I just hold my breath and wait. But always she comes through in the end. She's like a sapling, young and strong. I can't think about her any more now, because *I* might break in half if I do. And besides, here comes Eddie, back from the airplane bathroom, tucking in the tail of his shirt and making his way up the aisle and back to me.

All right, now *I'm* the one in the tiny bathroom, crouching in here on the toilet while the plane does a little vibration number from side to side and the RE-TURN TO YOUR SEAT sign goes on briefly.

I've never been afraid of turbulence. Not in any area of my life whatsoever—be it physical or emotional— and I'm not going to start being afraid now. I can't write this in front of Eddie. There's no way that I could let myself be free enough to get down on paper all the things that have happened if he was peering over my shoulder. One of those things would shock him, would completely throw him.

But I'll start with what happened to me on my way out of Springfield. Let's just say I took a detour, which is pretty much how I'd describe my entire life.

Eddie had come back with my stuff from the Spauldings' house. I was all set to go. I'd been forced out of town, and I was pretending it was all well and good, but inside, I was in pain. I still can't get over the look on Phillip's face when he told me to leave. He was, of course, angry but more than anything he was hurt; hurt that Beth was really dead, and hurt that he had fallen in love with her imposter.

Phillip could no longer stand the sight of me. I stood

for everything he hated: deceit, greed and lost love. His rejection of me was absolute. He would not reconsider. There would be no appeal. Like a body punch from Rayford, it was as if the air had been pulled from my lungs.

I hadn't known how bad I would feel until the moment he kicked me out. It took that action to reveal to me what I'd felt all along. *Need.* A need for Phillip. A deep and searing need that I can't possibly explain, and even more to the point, Eddie CANNOT know about, and so here I am hiding in the bathroom of a jumbo jet. Stealing a few minutes of privacy from Eddie so that I can write down my thoughts, release my pain. I haven't slept well. I'm a wreck. Eddie's being great, he's being wonderful, in fact, he's behaving just right, and I'm grateful to him. But it doesn't take away my sense of loss.

I keep seeing Phillip and how he looked when he told me to leave. I've known more than my share of pain and loss in my life, but never like this. It was not just the loss of Phillip. It was the sense that I was losing a life.

My thoughts keep going back and forth between Eddie and Phillip. It's like a deck of fifty-two cards, but with only two different cards, the Jack of Hearts and the Jack of Spades. No matter how I shuffle or cut the deck, only those two cards turn up, Jack of Hearts, Jack of Spades, back and forth, back and forth. One card I want, the other I need.

There was Eddie back in Company, holding up a one-hundred dollar bill he'd bummed off Phillip. And I showed him the blank check I'd managed to scam off of Phillip's father, Alan, earlier, in a final, one-for-the-road grift. Eddie was speechless and wanted us to get the hell out of there right away. I agreed, but not for the reasons he thought. I just wanted to *escape*—nothing more.

I'd been totally shattered. I'm shattered still, but I'm managing. Broken people can go far in life; they can straggle along and no one knows they're broken, no one has a clue.

Like Eddie. He has no idea, not a clue. He thinks that he's taking to Colorado a perfectly good, in-one-piece Lorelei. In fact, what he's got is something entirely different. I'm me, but barely.

Phillip doesn't want me. I disgust him; I make him sick. Who would have thought this would make me feel like I want to die?

Amazing how you can live inside your own skin for decades and still be shocked at your reaction to something so basic. My longing for Phillip is like a plant's need for light. I want to turn toward him the way plants do toward the sun. But he's turned away from me. Completely away. He's taken the sunlight with him, and I'm on this damn airplane with dependable Eddie who's proven himself to me, who wants to go the distance with me.

Now someone is knocking, pounding, needs to use the bathroom, says I've been in here forever and what's my problem?

Wait just a sec.

There. I just opened the door and yelled *"I'm . . . not . . . done!"* at a lady with a face-lift so tight she could barely blink her eyes, and now I'm back.

As I was saying . . .

There was the day we were leaving town. I was taking a leap of faith and going forward, but in fact I was dying inside. Dying completely, and Eddie had no idea. He thought I was fine, A-okay, that I was glad to be starting my life with him. Okay, let him think that. Partly, it's true. But I couldn't bear to leave Lillian and the children and, of course, Phillip. It isn't called "leaving" someone, though, when he's the one who wants you gone. Phillip wanted me gone; wished I had never been there, in fact. And, part of me agrees.

Get out of my life, Lorelei, was what he'd been saying. *Just go.* So I was falling apart now, practically crawling out of town with Eddie, and we stepped out of Company, into the cool night air of Springfield.

And then the cops were on us.

It happened so fast, I couldn't believe it. It took me totally by surprise, they grabbed Eddie first and they locked a set of handcuffs on him and were dragging him away. Someone grabbed my wrists, too, and clamped a set of cuffs on me. The cold metal dug into my skin. I remember some Indian finger-cuffs from when I was a girl; they're made of straw, and the harder you pull your fingers out, the tighter they get. This is true of handcuffs. The more you try to get away, the more bruised and raw you get.

Keep cool, Lorelei.

Calm down.

Take it easy.

I tried to tell myself these things. I tried to stay calm, but I wasn't calm. The world was falling apart around me; it was like buildings were collapsing everywhere. The sky was coming down. I tried to call on every piece of sanity I could find in myself, but nothing responded. I felt like there was a siren inside me, screaming and screaming.

Or was that me?

Now here's where it starts to get hazy. I have these moments where I lose time. I don't know how to explain them exactly. They feel like little seizures. Moments where I'm forced out of myself. Jerked up from my life. And time just falls away, tumbles away from me, and I'm not sure if it's been minutes or hours. Sometimes I'm somewhere else when I wake up. No, "wake up" is the wrong phrase—I haven't been asleep, really. I don't know where I've been.

It scares me; it makes me feel I am crazy, but I know I'm not. There was a disturbed woman at the homeless shelter in Chicago, and she walked around and around the church basement all night, talking to herself, saying things like, "Don't you bother me, Louie. Don't you give me any of your lip. Because I'll bust your face if you try to cross me, I swear I will." And then she would shadow-box, and it seemed as if she thought this Louie person was right there in front of her, and they were interacting and everything, and she was living a life with him, when in all likelihood she hadn't seen him in years.

Maybe he was dead.

Maybe he'd never existed.

Everyone has their own inner world of pain and illusions. I know I have mine.

The first time the seizure thing happened, I was at Company. Eddie was talking, telling me how he wanted to leave town and start a new life all over again, and the next second he was still telling me the same thing, but it was like I *missed* something in the middle. Like

208

when I was a girl in Albemarle and I'd be dancing around the trailer to a new C & W record I'd bought at Woolworth's with all the money I'd saved up, and I'd accidentally bump up against the record player— the pink Close 'n Play I'd gotten from my mama for my seventh birthday. And the needle would jump and the record would skip. One second, somebody's singing about their dog that got run over, the next second they're wailing about their cheating wife. It was like that all over again, only I couldn't go back and start the record over.

Whatever I missed, I missed.

After the first time it happened, I tried to forget it. I pushed it away just like I've pushed away every bad memory of my entire life. Just like I tried to push away Rayford with his stinking breath and big belt buckles, and just like I tried to push away my last moments with Jackson and Roberto.

The flight attendant is knocking on the door now. I'll have to go back to my seat.

∽

I'm back. Eddie's fallen asleep again. You'd think he didn't have a care in the world. Where was I? Oh yeah,

Eddie and I were being arrested.

God, that ride to the police station was humiliating. Sitting there in the seat with cuffs on, my hair in my face, people talking all around me, everyone speaking in an excited voice, and throughout everything there was the chemical scent of the pine-tree air freshener in the police car—the little cardboard pine tree that swung back and forth as the car rounded a corner.

What was the hurry? We weren't murderers. *We're just grifters*, I wanted to scream, but I had no voice, nothing. Then the station house, with some cop taking off the cuffs and another one grabbing my hand and jamming my thumb down onto an ink pad for fingerprinting.

There's so much shame attached to the black thumb. You can't get the ink off for a while. You sit there with your thumb a deep black color, like you've stuck it somewhere you shouldn't have. Like you're bad, which you are, for why else would you be getting booked and fingerprinted at the police station?

But worse than that, far, far worse, was when Lillian came to see me. She shouldn't have come there—I was so ashamed. She walked in and demanded to know what they had done with her daughter, and then she demanded to see her daughter.

Her daughter.

Me.

Yeah, right.

I was being tested, I swear that's what it was. Because it was like a knife twisting inside me, seeing Lillian in the station house and hearing her voice, the voice of a mother. When I heard her, I wanted to go into her arms, to have her say that everything will be okay, just like a mother's supposed to do. Just like my mama couldn't do. At least not when Rayford was around. But Lillian did that for Beth, I bet, and she thought she was doing it still. She would have done anything for her daughter. She would have thrown herself off a cliff if it would have given Beth a chance to live. She was a mother lion, defending her cub.

No, she was just a *mother*.

If I was a mother, that's what I'd do.

If.

Maybe I was. Maybe I am. I have that memory of a crib with a mobile turning above it, panda bears sitting on pillows. The haunting music of a nursery—sometimes it plays inside me from out of nowhere, and it makes me want to run out into the street and look for my baby, screaming "Where is she?" to anyone who will listen.

No one would listen. They would think I was mad. Lillian would listen. She would listen to anything I said, because she'd think I was Beth, and she knew that she and Beth were bonded for life. They were joined. Beth had grown inside of Lillian, getting bigger and bigger and being born. Emerging into a world full of pain, a world that sometimes becomes impossible to live in, but then where can you go?

You go back to mama. The only safe place. And mama was there—*Lillian* was there—in that police station, and I wanted to go to her, but I wanted to keep her away from me, too. I was pulled both ways, a tug of war, a tug of life.

I tried to get Lillian to leave, to walk out and go home. But she wouldn't do it. She insisted that her daughter was being kept in prison falsely, and that she wanted some answers, now.

I told her the truth. I told her who I was, loud and clear, but it was like my voice got swallowed up inside the roar of her own outrage. "Lorelei Hills" meant nothing to her; it was just a bunch of syllables.

I tried and tried to get her to believe me, telling her every detail, doing whatever I could to get through to her, but it was like my *words* were vapor. Nothing I said was real. I swore to her I wasn't her daughter, but it was useless. She thought I was confused. In need of help. She thought I was out of my mind, and maybe I am, but not the way she thinks.

I have had something happen to me that makes me think I am losing my sanity.

I can't go into it yet. It's too hard. I don't really understand it.

Focus on Eddie, Lorelei. He's real, he's yours, he's sitting next to you, fast asleep.

Eddie and I have been together for so long now. Even in jail we were together. He really tried to take care of me in there, too, just like he did in Mexico. He protected me from everything, he just couldn't protect me from myself.

It all began when they took him away for more fin-gerprinting. I started to feel panicky; I couldn't breathe, I was falling down the rabbit hole again. They'd taken my diary away. I mean, they took my purse, and my diary was inside.

"We'll need your belongings," was what they said, and someone took my purse, and then when I got into the cell I realized my diary was in there, and I thought, *Oh God, I need it back. I need it back now.*

With my diary locked away in some locker behind a sergeant's desk, I couldn't write in it. My outlet was gone. The thing that's kept me sane all along, the thing that's helped me get by from day to day, remember who I was, wasn't there. I felt frantic. Anxious. I needed my diary.

But I was trapped in that cell. My freedom was gone. I looked all around at the bars and the bare walls and the tile floor, and it was all unbearable to me. *Unbearable.* I needed to get out.

And then a door clanged shut. The sound rang in my head like a bell, echoing forever, and it made it happen again. *It.* You know. That experience I had in Mexico where I was having memories that weren't my own.

This time I saw a tower. And I was inside, looking out. I was imprisoned, just like in the jail cell. I was looking out at *Eddie*, for some reason. He was in the doorway and he was pushing me inside, his face twisted with rage. And then the door closed, and I was alone.

Alone in the tower. Isn't this where Phillip told me Eddie had once locked up Beth?

Other things came and went, too. Alan showed up in that tower. Or was it the holding cell? I really didn't know, couldn't tell fantasy from reality. It all blurred together. I was trapped. Inside the tower, and inside the jail cell. And then, suddenly everything was clear again. I felt like me again. Except I'd lost time.

Eddie was back. He was right across from me, pacing the cell. He didn't seem to notice anything had happened so I tried to act normal. I talked to him, and eventually I slept.

More dreams. Beth's wedding day. The marriage to Phillip. It was so real, I could swear I was there. I saw the guests, dressed to the nines, and the Spaulding mansion, all decked out for the occasion. There were flowers everywhere. It was Valentine's Day. Beth's birthday. Beth's wedding day. Except it's also my birthday, my wedding day.

I feel the veil whisper against my cheek, and my heart is beating so hard when I turn to look at Phillip.

He's gorgeous. He's mine. I'm aching for him, and I've got him, and everything is flooded with light. I'm going to spend my life with this man, this hero. My warrior. The man who will fight for me. I'm trembling so hard and the blood is rushing in my head so hard that I can barely hear the minister speak. I'm just about to say "I do" when Eddie wakes me.

He gave me a cupcake for Valentine's Day and told me he was going to go meet with the public defender.

Then the most shameful thing of all happened. Lizzie showed up at the holding cell. She called me *Mommy.*

It just about killed me, hearing that word. A cop let her into my cell and she threw her arms around my neck. She felt so good to me. I touched her hair and I was back there, in that vision again, the one where I was brushing a little girl's hair. The little girl was jabbering away and I was completely happy. She turned to face me and everything went white. Then there is nothing, I remember nothing else from my visit with Lizzie. More lost time.

My next memory is Phillip coming to the cell. He was angry at me for leading Lizzie on when she came to visit me. He said I told her I was Beth. I was confused. I didn't know what he was talking about. Things got fuzzy again, then white, then nothing.

When I came to, Phillip was still there. He acted as if nothing had happened. He told me he'd post my bail if I stopped pretending to be Beth and if I'd leave Springfield.

Leave. Leave. It killed me that this was what he wanted. He was standing so close to me, this man I could have been with forever, this man I could have made love to so powerfully, feeling our two selves merge as our bodies touched and joined. He hated me but he was confused, too. He didn't know what to think; he was lost, and so was I.

The plane is approaching Denver. Soon, Eddie will wake up, so I'll stop writing, for now, diary.

❦

Finally, I'm back on earth. The plane has landed in Colorado and here I am at the baggage carousel, waiting for Eddie to fetch the luggage. The carousel hasn't started moving yet, and everyone is just standing there.

Why do they call it a carousel? It's got nothing in common with the kind of carousel that little kids ride on. Both go round and round, but that's all. Kids laugh and shriek, so happy and excited, when they ride those horses. I can picture Lizzie on one of the horses, grabbing for the brass ring in the center, reaching out her little hand and trying to pull it toward her. But these people here in the airport aren't excited. They're not kids. They've been traveling, and now they're tired.

Like me and Eddie.

Oh, now the thing has started moving. Just look at Eddie, standing over there looking at the boring sight of a lot of suitcases moving slowly in a circle, rumbling all around, waiting to be picked up and lifted off the carousel and carried out of the terminal. Look at him there, standing and waiting, his eyes looking so tired.

Who is this man? He's supposed to be my life now. He's supposed to be *it* for me. I could pretend that he's everything I want. I could pretend that I've come to the end of the rainbow and there he is, the pot of gold, shining and glimmering and just waiting to be picked up and taken home. I could pretend that I don't miss the way Phillip kissed me. The feel of his lips on mine, the way they pressed against me so hard and soft. I could pretend and pretend until I'm blue in the face from pretending, but it wouldn't make it real.

You can't take a lie and make it true. Not even the best con artist in the world can do that. I know I can't.

The thing is, I need Eddie. He's my whole life now, my salvation, and the only way I'm going to make it in this world is with him beside me, guiding me through. He's the only thing that's keeping me going, keeping me alive.

I need to be good to him. We've been through so much together. What a long way we've come since that day on the bridge in Chicago when he tripped on a bottle and something made me go to him and help him.

We've been like two forces moving toward each other mindlessly. Following some instinct coded inside us, buried so deep we'll never find it. I guess I should feel that as long as I'm with Eddie, I'm home. But guess what? I don't feel it, no matter what I do.

What's wrong with you, Lorelei?

I don't feel much of anything lately. Those seizures— or whatever you'd call them—they've taken a lot out of me. Back and forth I went after I got sprung from jail, after they gave me my purse, with my diary safe inside. Back and forth between real world awareness and intervals of lost time. I remember only a few things. How I gambled our money in a pick-up card game at a pool hall and lost it all. It was the fever that did it; my head was a furnace, and the fever was stoking it. I got hotter and hotter; my mouth was dry as wool. My breath was sour, and my hair felt unclean, like I hadn't washed it in weeks.

I sat in that pool hall and drummed up a game. Some men were standing around one of the tables and I came in and sidled up to them with a deck of cards.

No one took me seriously; they wanted me out of there. I was a woman, a chick, a *girl*. Just a girl. I was p.o.'d that they weren't interested, and I wheedled and coaxed and begged, and they finally put their pool cues down and came around.

What a waste of time. What a disgrace. They took my money, and they laughed at me with their mouths open, showing bad teeth, and when I was done I was cleaned out, totally empty-handed, and no one had a scrap of sympathy. It was like: *What did you expect, coming in here where you're not wanted?*

Which made me think of Phillip all over again.

You can't make someone love you when he doesn't. You can't force it. It's square-peg-and-round-hole time.

And you can't force yourself to love someone who you don't love. Only I *do* love Eddie, I really do. Love comes in sizes. Large, Extra Large, Supersize.

After that terrible game in the pool hall, I went back to the jail to see Eddie, who was still locked up. And I had to confess to him what had happened, that the money was gone, that we had nothing. Oh, the look on his face . . .

But the thing was, I didn't even care very much. Because this was when I first started to get sick. I rested my head against those cold metal bars like they were an ice pack. I felt my stomach churn and my sinuses fill and my world start to spin. I promised Eddie I'd get the money back, and I know he was angry, but I felt like I wasn't even part of the conversation, like I was totally detached.

I left the jail again and went to Company, thinking

maybe I could find a card game there or something—but no luck. I didn't have any money and I was out of my head with fever. A waitress took pity on me and shoved a bowl of the soup du jour my way. I had no pride left, none whatsoever.

Then there were voices coming through the fog of my sickness, and Alan and Lizzie were there. I had to go to Lizzie. I had to. But Alan was in my face, furiously telling me to stay away from her.

Stay away from Lizzie? The little girl I loved? How could I do that?

My little girl.

But she wasn't mine, not really.

And then everything went white again. After that, nothing. No memories, no dreams, no thoughts of any kind. I lost time again, but not minutes, this time I lost days.

Somehow I wound up at the Spaulding mansion; all roads don't lead to Rome, they lead to Phillip. I found out later that he took me in and put me to bed.

I was just a shell of myself. A husk. Going in and out of reality, clinging to life but feeling dead the whole time. I stayed in bed, delirious, shaking, talking to myself like that crazy woman in the shelter, losing time. When I finally came out of it, Eddie was there. He and Phillip were arguing. That's the first moment I realized how much time I'd really lost. Eddie was out of jail; I was in Beth's bed. I couldn't account for any of this. I felt frightened. I didn't understand what had happened to me. I still don't.

The only thing I do understand about that whole time is that Eddie was there for me. He came *through* in the end, and that's the important thing. So I'm going to come through for him, too. It's the least I can do for both of us, because we need each other. I've got to remember this; I've got to remind myself of it every day, because it's true.

But if it's so true, then why do I have to *remind* myself? Why don't I automatically know it?

I don't even know what I know anymore, if you want the truth. And I'm tired of trying to figure it out. Right now I'd just like to toss this diary onto the baggage carousel, to let it slowly spin round and round, ignored forever, and then walk out of the terminal without it and start a new life. Because this diary makes me remember how much I have to keep figuring out. How much still makes no sense, even now, here in Colorado, far from the choking, claustrophobic world of Springfield, a place where everybody knows everybody's business.

Here in Colorado, it's just Eddie and me. The two of us and a silver mine. We'll go out there and look around the place, getting our bearings, seeing what the spread looks like, and we'll claim it as our own. Eddie and me. Me and Eddie. I'll keep saying this to myself, getting used to the words, because I'm going to be saying them for a long, long time.

෴

Okay, diary, Eddie's just picked up our bags and he's searching for one of those carts, and in a few seconds he's going to be over here and that'll be that.

So now I have to finally get it out. The weirdest thing of all. The thing that I've been hinting at but have been unable to write about before. I can't make any sense of it whatsoever.

It happened when I was finally alone in the bedroom at the Spauldings', after Phillip dragged Eddie out of there.

I haven't told a single person about it. But I can finally tell you, diary. I didn't judge it when it happened. I just let it happen, because there was no other choice.

I was pacing around the bedroom. Still sick but on the mend. I was preoccupied with questions about how I got here and the time I could not account for. Suddenly I heard a voice in the room. I'd thought I was

223

all alone. Who was here? Maybe a nurse or something?

I turned in the direction of the voice, and what I saw sent a chill through me. I haven't recovered yet.

I still keep thinking of how the voice said my name out loud. And it was coming from the *mirror*.

I looked across the room, and there in the mirror was a woman. She looked like me but she wasn't me. Not at all. I raised my hand but she didn't raise hers. She kept totally still.

I stared at her. She terrified me. I felt a chill spread across my body, but I didn't move a muscle, I didn't do anything. I just stayed there and waited while she introduced herself.

"Beth Raines," she said.

Here's Eddie with the cart. Time to go with him through the doors of the airport and out into our first day in Colorado. I won't tell him any of this. But I'll tell you, dear diary, first chance I get. I'll tell you everything, I promise. For now, though, it's time to leave the airport and start a new life. I'm battered and weary, but I'm still in one piece. Wish me luck.

～⌒

This is the first minute I've had to myself since Eddie and I got to Colorado. We've checked into this rinky-dink hotel called the Silver Slipper, and he's in the shower now, so I'll have to make this quick. But it hardly seems fair, there's so much to say, so much for me to try to figure out. So much I haven't had even a moment to think about. So much that Eddie doesn't know about me—and, I'm starting to realize, that I don't know about myself.

It was his idea to come to Colorado. He kind of slapped himself on the forehead and wondered why he hadn't thought of it sooner—that we could just get out of Dodge and head out to Colorado and collect on the silver mine that was Beth's rightful inheritance. It's not like I don't have enough pieces of identification to convince the local authorities that I'm Beth Raines. Or should I say local *authority*. You've heard of a one-horse town? Silver Springs, Colorado, turns out to be practically a one-*man* town, at least if you're someone who needs to get something done in an official capacity. The manager of the hotel where we're staying told us that he doubles as the town registrar, so he's the one who has to give my photo I.D. the once-over before handing me the title to the mine, and then he told us that he could also be the foreman in charge of putting together a crew to go into the mine to see just how much silver it holds. According to him, there's plenty of silver in there; the problem is getting it out.

And just where are we supposed to get this money? Don't laugh, but Eddie and I have put together a lounge act, and we tried it out tonight, right here at the Silver Slipper. You see, this hotel has a mind-reading team that wows the locals—or *had* one, anyway, right up until the moment today that they split up and went their separate ways, right in front of Eddie and me. Well, let me tell you, it wouldn't have taken any mind-reader to figure out what the two of us were thinking when we saw the two of *them* storming out the door. Eddie and I paid a little visit to our friendly neighborhood clerk/registrar/miner and talked our way into the gig. And as they say in show biz, we knocked them dead.

We worked out a code beforehand so we could signal each other—for instance, when I'm blindfolded and Eddie's holding up a key or a wallet that belongs to someone in the audience. But the fact is, Eddie and I really *can* just about read each other's minds. We really do make a good team, and I don't just mean on the postage-stamp stage at the Silver Slipper.

Ever since we've landed here in Colorado it feels

like we're meant to be together—which, as I've said, is just what I want Eddie to think. The difference now is that sometimes, it's just what I think, too. The more I'm with him, the more possible it seems.

Like tonight. We went for a moonlight walk through the snow to see the mine. I just needed to see it; I needed to make it real. And when we got there, it was even more magical than I dared imagine. Standing with Eddie, looking at the mouth of that mine reminded me of who I was. I decided right then and there that I was going to close the book on Springfield. No more pining away for Phillip and my lost family. I can't go back, I can only go forward. If my life proves anything, it's that. And Eddie is my forward, my future. Maybe we'll spend the rest of our lives together. Maybe he's my destiny. I think he feels it, too.

Even now, as I write these words, I get goosebumps: "the rest of our lives together." We leaned into each other, huddling against the cold, cherishing what we'd found with each other. We'd come so far, and we'd experienced so much, and now we would survive together forever. Because that's what the two of us were, more than anything else—survivors. That's what we had in common, that's what drew us so close that in time we wouldn't even need to work out a code beforehand to read each other's minds. That's what we've come back here, to our room, to celebrate tonight, all night, as tenderly as our hunger for each other will allow.

That's what Eddie allows me to remember about myself: I'm a survivor. And right now, that's what I need to remember more than ever.

Because there's more to this story. There's a dark side. There always is, isn't there? At least there is in my stories. But this dark side scares me more than anything else I've experienced because I can't run away from it. I've run from gunshots, step-daddies, rabbit holes and dreams, but I can't run from this. No, the only way I can save myself from this is to hold onto Eddie and to hold onto you, dear diary. You see, you're the only way I know I have a past and Eddie is the only way I know I have a future. He's like an antidote, he keeps me alive.

But the fact is, I can't let Eddie know this. I can't let him see just how dark my dark side is. Sure, he knows I was sad about leaving Springfield. He's caught me looking at pictures of Lizzie and James, and he couldn't possibly have missed the ache in my face. But what he doesn't know, what I can't let him know, is the real reason I jumped at the chance to go away with him. As much as I wanted to stay in Springfield, I had to get out of there, too. I had to be anywhere but Springfield, and fast. For me, it was a matter of survival. Because that town wasn't big enough for the two of us.

By the two of us, I mean Beth and me.

At first, when I saw her staring back at me from the mirror in her bedroom at the Spauldings', when I heard her saying who she was, I thought maybe it was the fever playing tricks on me. Then I thought that playing Beth for so many months had finally taken a toll on me. Then I thought I must be losing my mind.

Or maybe I'd already lost it, long ago. I mean, let's face it: I woke up in a bed in Mexico, not knowing who I was or where I was or how I got there. Since then, I've managed to piece together a good portion of my identity, but nowhere near all of it. Given everything I've been through, if I suddenly found out that Lorelei Hills was certifiably insane, I guess it wouldn't exactly shock me.

So, at first, I did what any reasonably sane—or even reasonably insane—person would do if she found herself staring at a mirror image of herself that wasn't moving like her, and talking to a mirror image that talked back. I simply figured it couldn't really be happening.

But it was.

Something was, anyway.

I tried turning away, but the voice followed me. *Beth's* voice, commanding me to look at her.

Something was *definitely* happening here, and whether it was inside my head or inside the mirror didn't much matter. Either way, it wasn't going anywhere. Not without me facing it.

So I did. I turned and faced her. Beth. Looking just like me, talking just like me—when I'm pretending I'm Beth. Only what she's telling me is that the reason I got so good at making her up is because *she* made *me* up.

She made *me.*

Lost in Mexico in more ways than one, she'd reached within herself and came up with someone who could help her. Me. Lorelei. And it worked, she said; I'd helped her. She learned how to be strong from me. And now she was telling me that she was ready to come back. And that I, therefore, would have to leave. As in vanish. As in cease to exist.

It was craziness, of course. Pure madness. On my part, on her part—it didn't matter, and I didn't care. Something was seriously out of control here.

And yet what she was saying made a crazy kind of sense, too. Even as I was telling her that she was talking trash—even as I was laughing in that pretty little face of hers at the idea that I would simply say okay, I won't exist—part of me was thinking, *What if she's right?* Because in that case, it would explain a lot. Too much, in fact. So much that all at once I thought that maybe I'd suspected as much all along, ever since the night I found Eddie on the bridge in Chicago, and he looked up at me and said my name. *Her* name, I mean.

And I don't mean just the obvious, weird coincidences. How I woke up in Mexico, and she disappeared in Mexico. How I've got gaps in my memory, and she's got gaps in her memory. How I look exactly like Beth Raines, and she *is* Beth Raines. How the sound of the mission bells triggered so many memories, sounds, tastes—even a new language. All these weird coincidences I'd already thought about a lot, but the fact is, life can be full of weird coincidences.

No, what suddenly made sense to me was that this is exactly what someone like Beth would do, if she found herself in a faraway land washed away in a flood, physically and emotionally. Wracked, drenched, swept along a gully and then burned badly under the unforgiving desert sun—who in that situation wouldn't want to be somewhere, or someone, else? She had been imprisoned in a tower, kidnapped, swept off her feet by the man she believed was her prince and then burned badly—wouldn't that be enough to push her past the breaking point?

Plus, losing Phillip. If this Beth Raines was anything like me, that might have been the worst part of all.

Losing Phillip and settling for Edmund: It would be like dying in your dreams, wouldn't it? Wouldn't she try to change the ending?

From what I knew of Beth, she wasn't someone who would give up without a fight. And the fight in this case involved reaching deep within herself to find a part of her personality—the part that wasn't much like Beth Raines at all—who could fight the fight for her. And if you're Beth Raines, the part of your personality that wasn't much like you at all might very well be . . . me.

So I admit it. I was beginning to have my doubts, even though I just kept telling that phantom in the mirror that she was full of it. But what cinched it was what she said next.

She asked me what I wore to my prom. What color was my dress. Who my date was. What make of car I drove.

Now, I could have told her to ask me questions I knew the answers to. Questions like: Who my mama was. What my step-daddy tried to do to me on my sixteenth birthday, and what he smelled like trying to do it. Who I played blackjack with in New York.

But I knew that it wouldn't have been any use. Because here I'd been, all along, trying to piece together the puzzle of who I am and who I was, and the answers I'd come up with couldn't be proven. There wasn't a soul in my past that could come forward and say I had existed. Everyone in my past had disappeared without a trace.

I had to get out of there. That's all there was to it. I threw a towel over the mirror just to shut her up and shut her *in*—inside whatever world she was. The time had come to get out of the Spaulding mansion and out of Springfield and as far away as possible from anywhere a memory of Beth Raines might be waiting in the shadows. Because if Beth was right, then maybe that's what would make her stronger. Being around the people who mean so much to her—her mother, and her children and Phillip.

So that's the real reason I'm here, dear diary. If I didn't get out of Springfield, I would have ceased to exist. And I couldn't have that. Because it's like I've said: I'm a survivor.

"Lorelei."

It was her again. Beth. Or the image of Beth. Whatever she was, whoever she was, she was back in the mirror again, only this time it wasn't the mirror in her bedroom at the Spauldings' but the one in the hotel room in Silver Springs, right after I wrote that last entry. Eddie got out of the shower and we ordered some champagne, but the bottle the hotel manager delivered was warm, and the ice machine down the hall was broken, so Eddie grabbed the bucket and went out on an ice hunt—or maybe a snow hunt. While he was gone, the manager asked me if I'd met up with my visitor.

Visitor? I said.

Sure, said the manager. Tall guy, good looking, sandy hair—Phillip, would that be his name? I sent him to meet you up at the mine. I hope he doesn't go in. Those old shafts are unstable, pretty dangerous.

I said it very well might be, and I pretended to call Phillip on my cell phone, just to get rid of the manager, and then I tried to put Phillip out of my mind.

But my mind wasn't cooperating.

Because that's when Beth showed up. Calling my name. Beckoning me back to the mirror.

So putting Beth out of my life wasn't going to be as easy as I thought. Just because I'd gotten as far away as possible from anywhere that had anything remotely to do with Beth Raines or the people she loved.

Wait a sec. Maybe that was it. Sure, I'd gotten out of Springfield. But hadn't Springfield followed me here? If my mysterious visitor was in fact Phillip, then maybe it was his presence nearby that was bringing Beth out.

It might sound like a wild theory, but if I had any doubts, they disappeared when I asked Beth what she wanted from me, other than to stop existing.

She said she wanted me to rescue Phillip. Now.

Fat chance, I told her. Did I really have to remind her that I was the strong one here, and she was the weak one? Go! Scram!

Well, she didn't scram. Instead, she folded her arms and gave me a look I hadn't seen in her before. And she told me that I was underestimating her. That she'd learned a lot from me about how to be strong. And now she was stronger than ever.

Which, I admit, spooked me a little. Because if she was as strong as Beth Raines and Lorelei Hills combined—well, I didn't want to think about that.

I tried again. Told her to get lost.

But she stood her ground. Just stared me down and told me to get out there and save the father of her children.

I covered my ears, but I could still hear her shouting.

"Go," she was shouting. "Go to the mine and save Phillip!"

I couldn't tell where the shout was coming from—the mirror, or me. But it was definitely inside my head, a piercing scream, whistle-sharp and blistering through me. I dropped to my knees and held my head. The shouting stopped, but not the pain. It felt like a bullet was passing through my head in slow-motion. I could almost track it, see it behind my closed eyes, a red streamer arcing across the midnight sky of my mind.

And then it stopped. In its place came a cool breeze, gentle and soothing. And silence. And something else—a feeling more than anything else, something I hadn't felt in quite some time, so long that I think I'd forgotten what it felt like.

Clarity.

I looked up and quickly got to my feet. I knew exactly what I needed to do.

I grabbed a coat and a lantern and headed out into the night.

"Phillip!" I called as I neared the entrance to the mine.

"Phillip!"

"Beth!"

It was Phillip's voice, coming from somewhere within the cave. I held out the lantern so I could see inside the entrance. Crazy shadows played along the walls as I tipped the lantern, trying to figure how far I could see, and whether it was safe.

I thought of running to get help. But then I thought of Phillip, needing me *now*—or else why wasn't he coming out of the mine on his own?

"Phillip!" I called.

It felt good, the sound of my voice, saying that familiar word, and knowing there was someone there who would answer to it. Someone who needed me as much as I needed him. Under the circumstances, maybe more.

So I said it again, and again, as I made my way into the mine. I picked out a path through the rocks and rubble and bits of wood on the floor of the mine and followed the sound of his voice until I rounded a bend and found a sickening sight: Phillip, pinned under a beam that had broken free of the ceiling.

I immediately set to work trying to free him. I placed the lantern on the ground and grabbed one end of the beam. A trickle of dust sprinkled us from the beams overhead. I shook it out of my hair and got back to working on the beam. I was going to save Phillip if it killed me.

He kept asking me to leave, to get out now, before the whole place came crashing down. Before the mine swallowed the both of us whole. But I wouldn't leave him there.

And he knew it.

He looked at me. Hard. Like he was seeing me for the first time.

Which in a way he was. Because now I was somebody I'd never been.

Yes, I was Beth, I told him, and he told me how

even though he'd eventually heard from the police in Springfield that my fingerprints matched Beth Raines's, he couldn't be sure what—or who—was waiting for him in Colorado. "Lorelei?" "Lorelei" pretending to be Beth? But the person kneeling beside him now was someone he almost didn't dare hope to find: Beth Raines.

But what he couldn't know is that I was more than the Beth Raines he knew. I was a better Beth than I'd ever been. It was almost funny, I thought, how all this time that I'd been trying to be someone I thought I wasn't—Beth—I was actually becoming someone I was: Lorelei. Here was a Beth Raines who was capable of rescuing Phillip Spaulding for a change.

Or was she? Was I? Because I have to admit, if I were really going to save Phillip I was going to have to do a better job than I was doing. I couldn't budge that beam. I stayed kneeling on the floor of the mine, resting back on my heels, studying the situation. I was going to have to get somebody else in here to help out. And then things got even worse. Just as I got to the entrance to the mine, something in the ceiling gave way with a tremendous *crack!*, and down came the metal door at the entrance. For a second I closed my eyes and stood completely still, convinced that the sound of the crash and its echo would be enough to send the whole place caving in on me and Phillip, burying us alive.

But when I opened my eyes, I was still there. Still alive.

Still Beth.

I made my way back to Phillip and told him that now our fate was in Edmund's hands. Which maybe wasn't exactly what Phillip wanted to hear, but it was our only hope. And even if Edmund never showed up and Phillip and I perished together, I think Phillip would have settled for that ending. Maybe it wouldn't have been a happy ending, but I think it would have been happy enough for him: the two of us back together. Phillip Spaulding and Beth Raines, sharing a common fate for all eternity.

I settled down on the floor of the mine, next to Phillip, and tried to make him as comfortable as possible. That night, I sat up a long time in that cold, damp, creepy place and thought about how far I'd come since the day I'd woken up in Roberto's big white bed in Mexico and asked myself: Who am I?

I *wasn't* Lorelei, that much was clear.

That person wasn't real—that Lorelei. She was a figment of my imagination, a phantom conjured out of all the trauma I'd experienced with Edmund—the kidnapping, and then the flood, and other events that I'm sure I'll start to remember over time. My mind just . . . shattered, I guess. It split apart because it would have been too difficult to keep everything together and face the facts of what had been done to me. And then when my mind began to rearrange itself, it took bits and pieces from my own past—like the idea of a mine, only this one was silver and Lorelei's was coal.

Roberto was real. That much I knew. But how much of the rest was imaginary? I couldn't shake the strange sensation that some of those people were flesh and blood—that they were people who actually existed, people whose lives touched mine.

It was possible. After all, there were periods of my life that I couldn't account for. What about Jackson Benedict? I could close my eyes, sitting there on the bumpy floor of the mine, and see the flash of a gun on a faraway morning as clearly as the light in the lantern.

Or what about that baby I pictured lying in her crib, with the panda mobile moving in a circle overhead? Who is she? Is she Lizzie? Or is she someone else altogether—another child of mine, somewhere out there in the world? If I insist to myself that she isn't real, that she doesn't exist, then am I just abandoning her forever, leaving her to a fate I can't even begin to imagine?

This thought is so disturbing it makes my head pound and my heart race, and finally I simply give in and stop thinking about it, because it's all too much to sort through right now. I'm Beth. I have my own children, and they're waiting for me in Springfield.

And yet, and yet.

I couldn't shake the feeling that somewhere, slightly behind me, looking over my shoulder, was Lorelei. And she was shuffling a deck of cards between her hands, and she was laughing.

I'm done with you, I wanted to tell her.

But I knew what she'd probably say:

Oh no, you're not.

Put it this way: If none of Lorelei's early life is real, then how did I learn to play cards and deal a hand so well? Nobody could just make that up. They'd have to be taught. How much of Lorelei's life actually happened? If I found out that some of it was real, I'd be frightened, but if I found out that all of it was imaginary, I'd be sad.

Because I *know* those people. They're Lorelei's history; they're her *life*. I was borrowing her essence for some time, living inside her mind when my own was too painful to inhabit. The personality of Lorelei, and all her emotional baggage and feistiness, made it possible for me to hide what had really happened to me, to cover it up with an entirely new personality and history—one that seemingly had nothing to do with my own.

But it did. The pieces somehow formed a picture of Albemarle, Virginia, and all the things that had happened there to scar me forever. I'd seen pictures of trailer parks, of course; one of them must have stuck in my mind, filed away for a time when I would really need it. And I guess I'd always secretly admired women like Lorelei—the kind of woman Beth Raines could never be, not in the polite society of Springfield. And when I was a girl, hadn't my own stepfather abused me? Raped me? Not Rayford—my real stepfather, Bradley, the one who left me the very mine I was now sitting in. Only in the Albemarle version, I changed the ending.

I looked up. Through openings in the top of the mine, I could see the stars. I thought of my trip to the planetarium. That was a real memory. The stars really do tell a tale of a brave warrior forever trying to rescue his princess. Of course, the warrior in the stars never succeeds but my warrior, Phillip, has rescued me. I had been trapped in Lorelei until he found me. Now I was free. Free to rescue him in return.

In the morning, first thing, Phillip turned his face toward me and I could read the look of concern there as clearly as the words on this page. I told him not to worry. That I was still me—still Beth.

And then he asked me a question I'd been asking myself: Was Lorelei gone for good?

The fact was, I couldn't be sure. How could I? But I had a feeling I was about to find out, because just then we heard a sound: Edmund's voice, calling my name—*a* name, anyway.

"Lorelei!"

Edmund came bounding around the corner. He stopped short when he got a good look at Phillip's unfortunate position. And, being Edmund, he gloated a bit. He grabbed my wrist, gave Phillip one last look and said it appeared that Silver Spring was about to lose a tourist this season.

But I didn't budge.

Edmund tugged me again, harder. But I held my ground, just like Beth did, in the mirror, back at the hotel.

"Lorelei—" he started to say, but I cut him off.

"I'm not Lorelei," I said.

He said I could drop the act now. But I told him it was no act.

"Lorelei?" he said. "What's gotten into you?"

He grabbed me by my shoulders.

"I'm not Lorelei!"

It was just like back in the hotel room. I heard the shout, but I couldn't tell where it was coming from. It was inside my head, anyway, that much I knew: inside my skull, piercing me, drilling away. I sagged in Edmund's arms, crumpling under the weight of the pain. And the truth is, part of me wanted to go with him in that moment, the Lorelei part.

Edmund pulled me.

I pushed.

I pushed again. Harder. Pushed him. Pushed Edmund.

"Lorelei," I heard him say.

I opened my eyes and leaned closer and looked right into his.

"*I . . . am . . . Beth . . . Raines,*" I said.

Edmund nearly tripped over himself backing out of there. Phillip and I could hear his footsteps fading into the distance, down the path toward the entrance to the mine.

What happened next was right out of a Hollywood fairy tale. Edmund slammed the door to the entrance closed, sealing Phillip and me inside—but in so doing he drew my attention to a metal bar that I was able to use as a lever on the beam pinning Phillip to the ground. I told Phillip not to worry—that I'd learned a valuable lesson in life: When you can't go backward, go forward. And then I led us away from the mine entrance until we found an ancient mining car on a pair of metal tracks, and we rode the car to the end of the line, and when we got there I reached up through the rocks and looked out from the darkness of the cave, and what do you think I saw, dear diary?

Daylight.

᳁

As I've been writing this, I've been on a plane some-where over America. This time it's not Edmund snooz-ing next to me under a thin blanket, but Phillip curled up on a leather chair under a satin comforter. We're on his private jet, flying back to Springfield from Col-orado.

Since getting out of the mine, I haven't been think-ing about the past much, for a change. Instead, I've been trying to concentrate on the future. When I get to Springfield, I'll go back to being a mother full-time; that much is certain—but *only* that much. Everything else, as I've told Phillip, is up for grabs. He offered to help me sort through it, but I shot him a look, and he got the message: Beth Raines—the new, and I hope, improved, Beth Raines—needs to do some things on her own.

In a way, I'm right back where I started, when I began writing in this diary. Who am I? Who is this new Beth Raines? How much Beth am I? And what part Lorelei? All I can say for certain right now, this moment, sitting on a jet where I'm literally up in the air, is that I'm both—and as I think everyone in Springfield will agree, that's plenty.

Author's Note

This book grew out of my work as an actor. When I work, I normally use a diary to help me understand what my character is thinking and what my character is feeling. I do this because, oftentimes, what people think and what they say are two different things. I believe it should be the same with characters on TV, in the movies, and on the stage. These differences are what give complexity and texture to the work.

In the case of Lorelei, I also wrote an entire back-story. I tried to write something that would be both parallel and in opposition to Beth Raines's life. I thought it would be interesting to create a character that had similar experiences but different reactions to those experiences.

In publishing this book, I give you personal insight into Lorelei, the character, as well as Beth Chamberlin, the actor. I hope you enjoyed your look behind the curtain.

All the Best,

Beth Ch L.